D0392974

"WHAT DO YOU THINK OF THE SHOW?"

Zoot looked around, not really seeing anything. He said, "I guess it's all for sale."

"Everything but the girl," Mr. Iron Will said, and laughed louder than the gag deserved. Still chuckling, Mr. Will said, "I think you could cause me a great deal of trouble, Mister Marlowe. I think now is perhaps a good time to stop you."

Zoot stiffened, expecting a couple of android goons to grab him. But Mr. Will just waved his hand over his head as if making a playing card appear.

On stage, Darken Stormy rolled off the Melt-O-Mobile and said, "You'll never have to park again!" She reached into the car and then backed away from it, making a here's-the-big-deal motion with her hands. The car began to evaporate and Zoot smelled credulity gas.

Mr. Will cried out, "This is Zoot Marlowe. He's a bad man. He deserves to die. . . ."

All around, people who had been ignoring Zoot looked in his direction with blood in their eyes.

They began to close in.

(0451)

WORLDS OF IMAGINATION

☐ **HAWAIIAN U.F.O. ALIENS by Mel Gilden.** A four-foot alien with a two-foot nose is sleuthing out a Malibu mystery. But it seems even a Philip Marlowe imitator might find himself and his duck-billed robot sidekick headed for disaster when he takes on spiritualists, thugs, and a Surfing Samurai Robot reporter. (450752—$3.99)

☐ **SURFING SAMURAI ROBOTS by Mel Gilden.** This first case of Zoot Marlowe's Earthly career would see him taking on everything from the Malibu cops to Samurai robots, motorcycle madmen to talking gorillas, and a misplaced mistress of genetic manipulation. (451007—$4.50)

☐ **STRANDS OF STARLIGHT by Gael Baudino.** A stunning, mystical fantasy of a young woman's quest for revenge against her inquisitors, and her journey through the complex web of interrelated patterns and events that lead to inner peace. (163710—$4.50)

☐ **THE MAGIC BOOKS by Andre Norton.** Three magical excursions into spells cast and enchantments broken, by a wizard of science fiction and fantasy: *Steel Magic, Octagon Magic,* and *Fur Magic.*

(166388—$4.95)

☐ **BLUE MOON RISING by Simon Green.** The dragon that Prince Rupert was sent out to slay turned out to be a better friend than anyone at the castle. And with the Darkwood suddenly spreading its evil, with the blue moon rising and the Wild Magic along with it, Rupert was going to need all the friends he could get.... (450957—$4.99)

Prices slightly higher in Canada.

Buy them at your local bookstore or use this convenient coupon for ordering.

NEW AMERICAN LIBRARY
P.O. Box 999, Bergenfield, New Jersey 07621

Please send me the books I have checked above. I am enclosing $_____
(please add $1.00 to this order to cover postage and handling). Send check or money order—no cash or C.O.D.'s. Prices and numbers are subject to change without notice.

Name_____

Address_____

City _____ State _____ Zip Code _____
Allow 4-6 weeks for delivery.
This offer, prices and numbers are subject to change without notice.

TUBULAR
ANDROID
SUPERHEROES

MEL GILDEN

A ROC BOOK

A BYRON PREISS VISUAL PUBLICATIONS INC. BOOK

ROC
Published by the Penguin Group
Penguin Books USA Inc., 375 Hudson Street,
New York, New York 10014, U.S.A.
Penguin Books Ltd, 27 Wrights Lane,
London W8 5TZ, England
Penguin Books Australia Ltd, Ringwood,
Victoria, Australia
Penguin Books Canada Ltd, 10 Alcorn Avenue,
Toronto, Ontario, Canada, M4V 3B2
Penguin Books (N.Z.) Ltd, 182-190 Wairau Road,
Auckland 10, New Zealand

Penguin Books Ltd, Registered Offices:
Harmondsworth, Middlesex, England

First published by Roc,
an imprint of New American Library,
a division of Penguin Books USA Inc.

First Printing, October, 1991
10 9 8 7 6 5 4 3 2 1

Copyright © Byron Preiss Visual Publications, Inc., 1991.
Cover Illustration Copyright © Byron Preiss Visual
Publications, Inc., 1991

All rights reserved

ROC IS A TRADEMARK OF NEW AMERICAN LIBRARY,
A DIVISION OF PENGUIN BOOKS USA INC.

Printed in the United States of America
Cover Illustration by David Dorman

Without limiting the rights under copyright reserved above, no
part of this publication may be reproduced, stored in or introduced into a retrieval system, or transmitted, in any form, or by
any means (electronic, mechanical, photocopying, recording, or
otherwise), without the prior written permission of both the
copyright owner and the above publisher of this book.

BOOKS ARE AVAILABLE AT QUANTITY DISCOUNTS WHEN USED TO PRO-
MOTE PRODUCTS OR SERVICES. FOR INFORMATION PLEASE WRITE TO
PREMIUM MARKETING DIVISION, PENGUIN BOOKS USA INC., 375 HUD-
SON STREET, NEW YORK, NEW YORK 10014.

If you purchased this book without a cover you should be aware
that this book is stolen property. It was reported as "unsold and
destroyed" to the publisher and neither the author nor the publisher has received any payment for this "stripped book."

For Ted Pedersen
Who is, as far as I'm concerned,
The Cat's Meow

Contents

Introduction

A vacation was only one of the things I needed, but it was also the only thing on the list that seemed likely. The other items involved having a lot of money or being taller. I was a little short of money because I'd bought a few cases of chocolate-covered coffee beans to take home to T'toom. I'd paid off my father with the profits from the first load and this time I was hoping to get a little ahead.

I was not only a little short of money, I was a little short. Period. I'm about average height for a Toomler, which is to say I come up to the average Earth person's navel. We don't have navels on T'toom either. What we do have is very long and sensitive noses. I'm the same unhealthy bone white as a mushroom. Only on T'toom, that's healthy.

The past few weeks had been educational. In a lot of ways, education was my business as much as trouble. I'd learned exactly how much damage Hawaiian UFO aliens can do if they put their minds, their talents, and their highly developed but unusual senses of humor to it. Like me, they were not of this Earth; but they were a little flashier about it than I am.

Since I'd solved the case, I'd been a busy guy, oh yes I had. What with eating pizza and drinking brewski and surfing my surf-bot by remote control, I don't know when I found time to think. Actually, I hadn't done much thinking lately.

I was filling time by sitting on the slouching couch in Whipper Will's living room spooning yoyogurt into my mouth. It was oat-bran flavor, the favorite that week. Whipper Will made the stuff himself in a special clean room at the back of the house.

The yoyogurt accounted for the halo of rainbows that surrounded everything, including the TV set and the Gino and Darlene movie it was showing. Surfers sprawled around the room, lively as moss. They ate yoyogurt and demonstrated varying degrees of interest in helping me watch the movie. At the moment, Gino was crooning a ballad to Darlene; it was called "Surfing the Stars" and was even sappier than it sounded.

Next to me on the couch was Bill, a silver robot in the shape of a duck. His legs lay straight out on the cushion—they didn't reach far enough to dangle. He came up only to where *my* navel would have been if I'd had one. It seemed to be only fair. We should all come up to each other's navels. (That was the yoyogurt talking.) Bill wasn't eating yoyogurt because he didn't eat.

I put down my bowl. I'd had enough yoyo-gurt. If the truth were known, I'd had enough of trouble and of surfers and of the wildly entertaining planet Earth. My sneeve was loaded with chocolate-covered coffee beans. For the moment, the only thing keeping me on the couch was inertia. I said, "Come on, Bill. I'd like to see you in my private office."

"Sure, Boss," he said and leapt to the floor. I stood up, not quite so steady as he because of the yoyogurt, and walked back along the dark hallway to the bedroom that Whipper Will shared with his girlfriend, Bingo. The bedroom smelled of humans and unwashed laundry, neither of which was a surprise. I led Bill around piles of linen in various states of cleanliness and told him to stand in the back of the closet.

"Right away, Boss." Though Bill was only circuits in a fancy box, I felt sorry for him, he was so eager.

I said, "I'm going home, Bill."

"Bay City?" He chuckled.

"Home," I said, and he nodded. I slapped a piece of flypaper on the top of Bill's head and the lights in his eyes went out. I turned him off every time I left Malibu for longer than a few hours. He didn't mind, and it kept me from worrying too much. I worried anyway. You never knew when one of the surfers might suddenly need something in the back of Whipper Will's closet.

I took off my brown double-breasted suit, my fedora, the rest of my Earth clothes, and hung them neatly in front of Bill. I put on my short johns, the rubber making a squeaky noise against my skin. I saluted Bill and walked through the house, not swaying much.

" 'Bye, dudes," I said to the surfers in the living room.

"Get down, Zoot!" Thumper cried with enthusiasm. He was the tallest of the surfers and made vague motions of being in charge when Whipper Will wasn't around, but generally he found leadership a bother.

I waved, then went out through the kitchen door, across the tiny brick yard, across the public walkway, and out onto the sand. The day was hot, and the beach was carpeted from horizon to horizon with blankets and towels. I could feel the heat pulling the effects of the yoyogurt out through my skin. The rainbows were fading.

Kids ran around, seemingly oblivious to the hot sand. Older folks—some maybe old enough to be in high school—strolled by holding hands or eating, sometimes showing a lot of talent and doing both at once. Most of the humans were lying on the beach, baking. Some were done. Others were only half-baked. That was a joke. If Bill were here, he probably would have made it himself. Or laughed. He was a handy audience.

Feeling steadier by the moment, I walked along the narrow slits of hot sand that showed between blankets, not attracting much attention. Whiffs of tanning lotion, sweat, and fast food pummeled me. I stopped at the high-tide

line and watched the water sparkle as it rose
and fell, heaving waves at the beach like a trav-
eling salesman heaving his suitcase onto a motel bed. Near me, a line of surfers ripped their
surf-bots pretty hard. Each surfer held a black
box in one hand and worked controls with the
other. Out on the water, robots—gold, silver,
bronze—cranked the waves top to bottom, while
their controllers hoped for that dream session,
that perfect ride through the crystal room. Few
of the surfers got wet any higher than their ankles.

I walked to a tall, dark human, a little older
than most of the other surfers. Near him was a
short, compact brunette. They showed a lot of
skin and were fairly brown, even by Malibu
standards. They were intent on their surf-bots
and didn't see me. I waited for the bots to glide
up onto the beach and grate to a stop. The bots
stood at attention on their boards while we
talked.

"I'm history," I said, surprising both of them.

"Coming back?" the man said. The brunette
smiled at me but didn't say anything.

I nodded and said, "Life gets dull in Bay City."

The man laughed as he shook his head at the
wet sand. Whipper Will knew the truth about
Bay City, and Bingo probably did too. It was
kind of like a joke between us.

Whipper Will said, "Wait a minute, dude. I
have something for you." He took a few steps
up to where the sand was dry and took something from a canvas bag. He came back and

handed me a paperback book wrapped in plastic. A mystery novel by Tony Hillerman.

"Going-away present," Bingo said.

I nodded and stuffed the package down into my short johns. "Bitchen," I said.

I shook hands with Whipper Will and traded hugs with Bingo. After a nervous moment, I turned to contemplate the ocean, letting waves make wings past my legs. The water was even colder than I imagined it would be.

I waved one last time to Whipper Will and Bingo, and plunged in and swam out to the saucer-shaped ship on the floor of the bay. It was my sneeve, the *Philip Marlowe*. Inside, everything was as I had left it. I popped a few chocolate-covered coffee beans into my mouth just for luck and blasted off.

On the ride back to T'toom I had plenty of time to go through the photographs I'd taken, to read the Hillerman and some of the other mystery novels I'd brought, to wonder if I'd actually return to Earth one more time. If I stayed on T'toom, my life as a detective was over. Trouble would no longer be my business. Perhaps my business would be applying household ooze or fixing slaberingeo spines or even looking for local substitutes for chocolate and coffee. But not trouble. Not the kind of trouble they have on Earth. My musings seemed to be very much like an answer to my question about whether or not I'd return to Earth.

I landed on T'toom and was met by the fam-

ily. My parents had gotten a little older since
I'd been there last, but Grampa Zamp looked
about the same and was as cantankerous as
ever. Although everybody had noses the size of
mine, they looked too big to me. I'd been on
Earth a long time. Because we'd been receiving
commercial radio broadcasts from Earth for a
while, we all spoke English. Almost everybody
on T'toom did. Fans of *Little Orphan Annie* and
The Shadow were everywhere.

Dad was glad to see more chocolate-covered
coffee beans. On my last trip home the demand
for them had been huge. He'd used some of the
money to pay for re-oozing the house.

I was not the celebrity I'd been last time. I
heard from a few biologists who wanted to
learn how the human body worked—things I
didn't know, things I doubted most Earth people knew. Mostly I was just Zoot come home
again.

I showed off my photographs after dinner that
night. My parents glanced at them and suggested I give them to some local scientists. As
usual, Grampa Zamp studied the photos as if
they contained winning lottery numbers and
asked me a lot of questions I answered in the
vaguest way I could.

Mainly, I stuck with my story that Earth was
a terrible place, a nest of monsters, each hun-
grier than the other. We both knew it wasn't
true, because last time I'd been home I'd told
him it wasn't true, but I needed the practice
and Grampa Zamp seemed to understand. I

don't know who I was protecting, but I did know that a lot of extra unidentified flying objects from T'toom would not look good in the skies of Earth.

After dinner Grampa Zamp and I went for a walk. The abo trees were dripping and far away we could hear a slaberingeo crashing through the forest. Familiar smells enveloped me: nothing quite as pungent as hot grease or chocolate, but pleasant flowery smells that came and went like daydreams. We didn't talk for a long time. I was getting used to being home and I think Grampa Zamp was letting me do it.

Other folks were out walking too. One of them stopped me cold. I looked after him as he continued on his way.

"Your mouth is hanging open," Grampa Zamp said.

I closed my mouth but I continued to stare. What I had seen was a Toomler with a nose like an Earthman's. A short blobby thing barely worth mentioning. It looked like a marshmallow in the center of the kid's face.

I said, "I guess I missed a lot while I was gone." Grampa Zamp took my arm and we started to walk again.

He said, "It started pretty soon after you left. Copies of those pictures you brought back were everywhere. Some of the wilder element decided that if they could talk like an Earth person, they should look like one too."

"They had their noses bobbed?"

"I hear tell it's the single most popular operation in the world." He shook his head.

I wanted to say something clever but nothing occurred to me. I was too horrified. Looking like an Earth person was not the same as talking like one. Whereas the learning of a foreign language was kind of self-improving, self-mutilation had never held much allure for me. "The wilder element has gotten a lot wilder since I went away."

Grampa Zamp nodded and said, "Earth is a popular place, considering nobody's been there but you." He looked at me kind of sideways, as if waiting for me to disagree with him.

"The charm of radio," I said, wondering what he was leading up to.

"Charm," Grampa Zamp said. He pulled some sap off an abo tree, rolled it between his palms for a moment, and pitched it into his mouth. He chewed mightily and went on, "I want to go with you next time you go there."

"Maybe I won't go again."

Grampa Zamp snorted.

"Besides," I said, "one Toomler on Earth is hard to explain away. Two might be impossible."

"I thought trouble was your business." He handed me some sap.

I rolled it as he had and sucked on it. It tasted a little like cinnamon. Durf, it tasted exactly like abo sap. Clouds of childhood memories gathered 'round. I said, "Earth people have plenty of trouble. They don't need more. *I* don't need more."

He looked at me as if I'd slapped him with a rolled-up newspaper.

"Look," I said. "You are probably my favorite person in the world. Any world. I am very happy when we are together, just hanging around chewing abo sap. But Earth really isn't the perfect vacation spot."

"I've been around, Zoot. I don't need to be coddled."

"No."

"I see. Greedy, ain't we?"

"No."

"I'll get my own sneeve."

Of course, he could. He didn't need me to take him to Earth. But I didn't think he would. In his mind, Earth had become my property and he would respect that. All that aside, if he'd wanted to go alone, he would have already gone. So I called his bluff. I said, "All right. Go ahead. But remember, Earth really is a dangerous place. Not only for Earth people but for us. If somebody from one of the colleges can convince the government you're not from their planet, you could wind up in a zoo—or worse, on somebody's dissecting table." He had the grace to shudder.

On the way back to the house, we passed another Toomler with his nose bobbed. Zamp and I just looked at each other and shook our heads.

I stayed around another few days, relaxing and filling up on home cooking. I would have stayed longer, but Zamp kept picking at me as if I were a scab. When I began wondering why I *couldn't* take Zamp to Earth, I decided it was time to leave. When I told Zamp he acted as if he didn't care. That was a clue with a search-light on it. I missed it just the same.

When I told my mother I was leaving, she said, "Again?" as if I'd astonished her.

"Unfinished business," I said, hating myself for lying.

My father asked me if I thought I was doing the right thing. When I said I didn't know but had to do it anyway, he said, "Don't forget to bring home more chocolate-covered coffee beans."

My sneeve was tanked, cranked, and ready to go. I got aboard and sighed, thinking about Zamp. I told the computer my destination and pushed the big button. Seconds later, nothing was around me but nothing.

I was sleeping and a sound woke me. It wasn't one of the chitters or clanks that the ship occasionally made; it was the squeak of a hatch opening. Raymond Chandler said that if you wanted to perk up your writing, have somebody enter a room with a gun in his hand. I hoped that wasn't happening to me. With my eyes still closed, I stiffened. Then another thought came to me and I relaxed. I said, "Everything all right, Grampa Zamp?"

"How'd you know it was me?"

I opened my eyes. He was smiling shyly at the

deck. He said, "You won't take me home, will you?"

"I'll do worse than that. I'll take you to Earth."

That brightened him right up.

I was angry with him for a while, but soon I worked it out. I had to admit that having company on the trip was an improvement, and Zamp and I had always gotten along. I was still certain that taking Zamp to Earth was a bad idea, but short of taking him home I could do nothing about it. Taking him home would be entertaining, but it would be trouble for everybody, mostly for me and Zamp.

I read to him from the Hillerman novel Whipper Will had given me. He liked the Indian stuff, but he couldn't make it match up with the things he'd heard on westerns like *Tom Mix* and *The Lone Ranger* and *Gunsmoke*. I tried to explain about reality, but he was determined to take the romantic view.

The sneeve slid into the ocean off Malibu and planed through the water to the bottom. I put my books away and shut everything down. I had only one pair of short johns and I let Zamp wear them. They would protect him from the cold a little. I, on the other hand, would freeze my big Toomler schnozz off. We stood in the airlock and let it screw us out into the cold salty water, which struck me like a hammer. We couldn't breathe underwater forever; I grabbed Zamp by the wrist and pulled him toward the shore.

We felt the slope of the beach and walked up

it and out of the water. It was late afternoon. The Sun was behind us and cast long shadows. Here and there diehard sunbathers were still staked out, but even as we watched, a few of them got up and headed for their cars. The air cooled rapidly. Grampa Zamp looked around, his nose twitching with excitement. Coming here with him was nearly as exciting as my own first arrival.

We walked across the sand, across the public walkway, across the small brick yard, and into the house. Everywhere Zamp looked was an eyeful of stuff he had never before seen.

"Hey, bros!" I called out. The house was empty.

"Is this normal?" Zamp said.

I shook my head. Then I heard shouting at the front of the house. I took a moment to pull on a pair of walking shorts that I found in Whipper Will's room and went outside. Zamp and I walked into a riot.

1

Sucking Sidewalk

People stood in tight knots on the postage stamp cement apron in front of Whipper Will's garage. They shouted at each other angrily and waved sheets of paper in each other's faces like revolutionary flags. Dress was the usual casual affair: bathing suits, sandals, T-shirts advertising brewski and surfboards. I recognized most of the people; they lived up and down Pacific Coast Highway—what passed for neighbors in Malibu. The surfers were out there too and more excited than I'd seen them since somebody had tickled their surf-bots with a sledgehammer.

"What are they doing?" Zamp said.

I had no idea. There was nothing like it on T'toom. I said, "Sports."

"This can't be baseball. I doesn't sound like this on the radio. Maybe it has something to do with us."

That was wishful thinking. Nobody was paying us any mind. I walked up to a blond woman who was wearing a bathing suit made from three tiny blue flags and asked her what all the hubbub was about.

She glared at me for a moment as if deciding whether or not to bite off my head. "Just look," she said, and shoved a white sheet of paper into my face. I took it and saw a neatly typed letter from a guy named Max Toodemax. It said:

Dear Renter,
     As you know, both property taxes and property values are soaring here in Malibu. Because of this, I find that it is no longer financially practical to rent single-family dwellings.
     These single-family dwellings will soon be replaced by high-density condominiums. You will be the first to be offered an opportunity to purchase one.
     Therefore, the Gramarcy and Mills Demolition Company will soon begin demolishing your house. The law requires that I inform you one month in advance. You may consider this your one and only notice.

                              Best wishes,
                              Max Toodemax, owner

"What does it say?" Zamp said.

"It says that any minute now you and me and all these nice people will be sucking sidewalk." I handed the paper back to the woman.

Whipper Will climbed onto something and raised his arms over his head. He said, "Hey, dudes. This hip-hop really has me dissed, dogged, and drilled, just like you. I mean, this is one grotty fall."

"Is that English?" Zamp whispered to me.

"We gotta, like, organize," Whipper Will said.

"Tell 'em, bro!" somebody shouted. I think it was Captain Hook, the surfer most likely to shout.

"But we need a plan, man. We gotta get our stuff wired."

"I nominate Whipper Will," a woman cried.

Somebody else called out his name and soon it was a chant. Whipper Will just looked perplexed. He waved his hands at the crowd as if testing the softness of a bed. The lights on PCH changed twice before the crowd got quiet enough for Whipper Will to speak.

"No way, dudes. Somebody had to throw down the rap about getting our stuff wired. I volunteered to rap, but I'm no kahuna. You'll need somebody more gnarly than me before you're done." Whipper Will stepped down and the crowd began to grumble to itself again.

Whipper Will and Bingo walked to the door followed by the other surfers. When Whipper Will saw me, he smiled as if he were selling teeth and cried, "Cowabunga!" He grabbed me and danced me around while the other surfers pounded any part of me they could reach. I was conscious of Grampa Zamp standing nearby wondering if I was being attacked.

"How they hanging, Zoot?" Thumper said.

We were attracting attention, so instead of answering I said, "I'll tell you about it inside," and kind of backed away from Whipper Will, hoping he and the others would follow me.

"What's this?" Captain Hook said. He hooked a thumb in Grampa Zamp's direction.

"He's with me," I said, making Captain Hook laugh. I kept moving, and pretty soon I'd attracted all the surfers into the living room with the front door shut against the crowd still festering outside. Nobody sat down, but just looked at me and Zamp as if we were what we are—a little bit unusual, a little bit not-of-this-Earth.

I said, "Tough times."

"Grotty for sure," Bingo said.

"What will you do?"

"Pray for surf!" Flopsie (or was it Mopsie?) cried. They were redheaded twins. Each surfer answered her with a mighty "Ahh-rooooha." Whipper Will shrugged.

Thumper, who had been looking between me and Zamp as if he were reading subtitles, said, "You mean there's two of you guys?"

"At least." Which could grow up to be a lie if I let it. "Bay City's a big place."

"How *is* Bay City?" Whipper Will said.

"They must be losing their grip. I still have the same head I left with."

Mustard, who was never entirely straight, cried, "Ahh-roooh!" and the other surfers helped him. Flopsie and Mopsie hugged me. Hanger went so far as to brush the tip of my nose with her lips. It was official. I was home.

"So," said Captain Hook, when the shouting had not quite died down, "who's the new bro?"

Whipper Will and Bingo watched me. Everybody watched me. Even Zamp watched me, but with a smile that was a little ashamed at having been caught playing in this neighborhood. He was enjoying seeing what the boy could do. I was on my own.

I said, "This is my Grampa Zamp."

"He have a problem with toxic waste and nose drops too?" Captain Hook flicked his own nose meaningfully.

I had pushed that explanation pretty hard the last time I'd come to Earth. I hoped a few more good miles were in it. I said, "Some of that environmental stuff made quite an impact."

Mustard made his victory noise again, but everybody else just looked confused. Hanger grumbled about pollution. Zamp's nose quivered; I only hoped he'd keep his mouth shut for a while. One lie that size was about all that would fit in the room.

"He speak English?" Captain Hook said, none too kindly.

"When there's any call for it," Zamp said, causing the surfers to stare at him as if he'd suddenly gone all normal. Whipper Will laughed and shook his head. "Another Chandler fan," he said.

Mopsie (or was it Flopsie?) astonished Zamp by putting an arm through his. She said, "Ever tried yoyogurt?"

"Get those short johns off him," Thumper said. "He needs some rad rags."

"O-o-o-o," said Hanger as if somebody had just tickled her fancy.

Zamp, hoping for guidance, looked at me as he was dragged toward the second bedroom. I called after him, "Relax and enjoy it." I remembered my first night in Whipper Will's house. They'd gotten me drunk on yoyogurt and brewski and we'd done the limbo till dawn. I didn't actually remember that particular dawn, of course. If Grampa Zamp had come to Earth for anything, it was this.

Only Bingo and Whipper Will and I were left in the living room. Bingo said, "Is he really your grandfather?"

"Yeah," I said. "I hope his hearts can stand the excitement."

"He's a gnarly old dude. He'll be cool."

I nodded and said, "Maybe it's not Grampa Zamp I should be worrying about."

2
Stormy Weather

The surfers decked him in baggies and a Hawaiian shirt. Captain Hook said something nasty about how groovy it was that not everybody from Bay City thought a brown suit and hat was the freshest fashion. I don't suppose Zamp looked any sillier in his outfit than I looked in mine.

A little light was left, a white luminous string at the horizon, so they half-carried Zamp out to the surf line and showed him how to use a surfbot. From the kitchen window, I watched him whoop and carry on. Earth was his oyster. Whatever an oyster was. I only hoped that oysters didn't bite.

When it was too dark to see, the surfers sat Zamp down with a Gino and Darlene movie and a bowl of oat-bran yoyogurt. After that they put on music not much louder than the wild cry of a slaberingeo and taught him dances for which I did not have names. Or they might just have been nervous conditions. I went to bed long before any of them were done. The last I saw of Grampa Zamp, he had a fishnet draped over his head and he was shaking his hips as if trying to dislodge a couple of flies.

The next morning I got my brown suit—the detective uniform—out of the closet. Bill stood behind it, right where I'd left him. I wasn't on a case. I wasn't going anywhere. Bill would just be in the way. But we'd been through a lot together and I had gotten used to him being in the way. Maybe I even liked it. The flypaper hissed when I pulled it off the top of his head. The lights behind his eyes came on and he said, "Hello, Boss."

"Hello, Bill. How they hanging?"

"They?" he said. "Hanging?"

"Forget it," I said. "Come on out of the closet."

Bill watched me put on the suit, then followed me to the breakfast nook and swung his feet up and back over the edge of a kitchen counter. Meanwhile I read the paper and drank coffee. The world was still having affairs. I didn't understand all the comics, but then, some of them probably weren't funny. I figured that as long as the artists continued to draw aliens that looked like sacks with eyeballs on the tips of their antennae, I was safe.

Zamp stumbled into the kitchen still wearing the Hawaiian shirt and baggies. They were a little wrinkled. He looked as if he'd had a wonderful time the night before and now regretted it. He collapsed into a nearby chair and held his head. I read the paper. He jumped every time I rattled a page.

At last Zamp said, "So this is Earth."

"Accept no substitutes."

"Last night was amazing."

"Don't try that stuff at home."

"Those guys are professionals?"

"No. Just Earth people."

"Yeah." A moment later Zamp said, "Nice clothes."

"The uniform. 'Trouble is my business.' "

Zamp chuckled and was sorry. He said, "I knew you were crazy for that Philip Marlowe radio show, but I didn't know you were this crazy."

I nodded and shrugged.

Zamp said, "So, what's pizza?"

Bill made a tiny mechanical guffaw. Zamp looked at him and said, "I don't believe we've met."

"That's Bill, my robot. He likes to shake hands."

Zamp shook hands with Bill for as long as he could stand it. "Pizza?" Zamp said.

"Nobody here by that name," Bill said.

While Zamp stared in surprise at Bill, I said, "I don't think you'd be very interested in it in your condition."

"Pizza is food?"

"More or less. It's good, but a little hard on the stomach."

He contemplated that. It was difficult work. After a night of brewski and yoyogurt and dancing, just circulating your blood was difficult work.

He went away and I finished my coffee and the comics. They did not become more comical. Flopsie, Mopsie, and Hanger came in and giggled as they poked through the refrigerator.

The morning was busy. I dozed in the sun for a while, helped Hanger pot a plant, and traded quips with Captain Hook before he went out to surf with his bot. I had a nice chat with Whipper Will and Bingo about their chances of stopping Max Toodemax from bouncing them. Bill's chance of becoming a nuclear physicist was better. With all that excitement, I could barely catch my breath. I could have stayed on T'toom.

Bingo and Whipper Will and I sat at the table thinking foggy gray thoughts about what kind of world it must be if a guy who has enough money can toss people out with the garbage. Suddenly Bingo cried, "Y-e-a-o-w!" and leapt to her feet. She scrambled to a drawer and pulled out a clutch of odd-sized paper—old envelopes, advertising, ticket stubs among them—and set them on the table before me as if serving a steak. "Messages," she said. "All from Knighten Daise."

If I'd had eyebrows, they would have gone up then. Knighten Daise and his daughter Heavenly had given me a lot of grief on my first trip to Earth. Them and their Surfing Samurai Robots. I thought I had done with them. I turned over the messages one at a time and saw a tossed salad of scribbles, each one of which told me Knighten Daise's name and phone number and the word URGENT, occasionally even spelled correctly.

I selected one of the neater messages and went to dial the number. The phone was answered by a low mellow voice that sounded too perfect to be real, and it was. It belonged to Davenport, the Daise robotler. I told Davenport who I was and that I wanted to speak with Mr. Daise.

A moment later somebody else came on the line speaking with a thick, heavy, gelatinous voice. "Mr. Daise?" I said, feeling a little goofy talking to it. If that was him, he wasn't using the hissy whisper he had when he was a lobster.

"Marlowe? Where have you been?"

"Away. Is there some problem?"

"I want you over here right now."

"Is there some problem?" I said again.

"Look out your window. Androids are everywhere."

I nodded into the phone and it had the expected effect. I stopped myself and said, "You have android trouble, Mr. Daise?"

"Must you always play hard to get, Marlowe? I'm offering you a job, and I want you to come over so we can discuss it."

Daise was right, of course. He didn't have to tell me what he wanted. I was ready to mow his front lawn if that was all he wanted. So far this trip had been as dull as a dirty window. Trouble was my business. Here was trouble. The fact that I didn't like Mr. Daise or his robots slowed me down a little. But I was bored enough to play his silly game, that was for sure.

I was about to tell him I'd be right over when Grampa Zamp came back into the breakfast nook looking less like a sick seagull and announced he was hungry. "Pizza," he said. It was not merely a suggestion.

Into the phone I said, "I'll be over tomorrow."

"Today, Marlowe. I've waited long enough."

"There are people ahead of you. You've taken a number. I'll be over tomorrow."

He huffed at me, finally agreed, and hung up. I felt better already.

"A case?" Whipper Will said.

"Not yet. So far it's just a phone call." I turned to Zamp and said, "Pizza?"

"That's what I'm told," Grampa Zamp said.

Whipper Will and Bingo were game, and I sent Bill down to the beach to see if any of the surfers were interested. Silly me. A surfer who was not interested in pizza was probably dead. We all strolled up the public walkway pretending that if everything did not suit us just so, we'd turn it into a parking lot.

Malibu was having another beautiful day; you can live there for a long time without seeing anything else. The ocean looked like a sheet of diamonds, but it still smelled like the ocean. The smell had to fight hot grease, thin chili, and tanning lotion, but it won. The ocean always does. The sky was so blue somebody might have trucked it in from Hollywood. It came complete with a hot white sun that might have been carved from a new kind of ice.

People who had nothing better to do were out in force. Enough more than a few of them wore the same unusual jewelry that I wondered if it was more than a fad. I pointed them out to Whipper Will.

"The blue plastic collars?" Whipper Will said as if I had insulted him. "Superhero Androids."

"Meaning?"

"Meaning vat-grown simulacrums of human beings. No springs, no gears, no electronics. Just android stuff. I understand that each of them has a particular superpower."

"Leaping over tall buildings in a single bound?" Zamp said. "Stopping bullets with their chests?"

Whipper Will almost smiled, but it died and curled up like a dead beetle and made a nasty snarl. Whipper Will was generally a cool dude. Snarling was not like him. He also seemed to have lost the surfer lilt to his voice. He had spoken an entire paragraph without using the words *dude, cool,* or *gnarly.* Bingo was looking at him worriedly, as if he were a stranger with frightening ideas.

Whipper Will pointed to an android taking a photograph of a mom, a dad, and two small kids. "See that? The picture that SA android is taking will be in focus, perfectly composed, and perfectly lit. That's one of their superpowers." He pointed to a couple of old folks approaching the public walkway. They were being led by an android who also carried two beach chairs, a small library of paperback novels, a cooler, and a big inflated duck. As they reached the walkway, one of the public trams came along and stopped right in front of them, allowing them to board. "Another superpower," Whipper Will said. "I don't know if they *make* public transportation come or if they just time everything perfectly. But somehow, if you're with an android and you want a bus or a taxi, you can always get one, and right now."

I said, "You sound pretty dogged by the whole thing."

"Dogged, yeah." He could not quite bring himself to spit. Instead he just curled his lip again.

A little nervously, Bingo said, "The blue collars identify Superhero Androids the way the forehead cloths identify Surfing Samurai Robots. The ads say the blue collars complement their beauty. You all right, Whipper?"

"Cool," he said. "Boss. Bitchen." His tone said he was none of those things. His thoughts did not make him happy but he continued to think them anyway.

Even walking together, Zamp and I did not attract much attention. Malibu was that kind of town. If we weren't making the cliffs slide onto Pacific Coast Highway or polluting the ocean, we weren't important.

Androids were everywhere. I saw more of them as we turned up a sidewalk toward PCH. Some people had robots following them, but not as many as I would have expected. Not as many as I'd seen the last time I'd been on Earth or even the day before. I wondered how Knighten Daise, the owner of Surfing Samurai Robots, was coping. Maybe I should have seen him today, after all.

I said, "What's that?" and pointed to a machine about the size of a coin-operated canned soda dispenser. It was painted in cool green and blue stripes and had a thick slot all down one side. Across the top it said Melt-O-Mobile.

"You'll see," Will said as if I'd be sorry when I did.

After that I noticed one of those machines on almost every corner.

The other surfers were not so polite as Whipper Will and Bingo. They made contemptuous barnyard noises at the androids. Bill got right into the spirit, of course. "Dorks," Mustard said. "Androids drill me bad. Not cool and gnarly like surf-bots." The other surfers agreed. Captain Hook added, "Hodads," and made the word sound as if androids never bathed or brushed their teeth.

As we approached PCH, I noticed a bad smell but it wasn't the traffic. It was like rotting slaberingeo spines, like dirty dishes that had been in the sink too long, like a factory where more people than the national average would be dying of some wasting disease. "What's that?" I said.

"What?" Whipper Will said. I was a little surprised he was not too preoccupied to answer.

"The smell."

"Something big and ugly is dead," said Grampa Zamp.

Whipper Will said, "I don't smell anything." Nobody else did either. Just me and Zamp. We had the noses for it.

We stopped at PCH and waited for the light to change. Every shop on the street was doing a brisk business. People who walked by had six or eight sunglasses hanging from their necks by cords, a hamburger in one hand and a taco in the other, and a box of fried chicken tight under their arms. T-shirts, rubber shoes, and souvenir clamshells also moved faster than hotcakes on skids.

Near us, an android pulled up in a small automobile that could have been a million others except that it had the flat lackluster look of something that had been assembled from a sheet of cardboard. Tab A in Slot A.

No parking space was there, but a couple of very young kids leapt out, followed by a woman with no more shape than a potato. "Do it," the kids cried, "do it," as they danced around like water on a hot stove. The android got out of the car, leaned back in through the open window, and hit something on the dashboard. The top of the car began to fizz; as it bubbled and popped, the top of the car evaporated.

The light changed, but we didn't move. We just watched as the fizzing spread quickly; soon the car was gone, up in nothing at all. The kids cheered. The dead smell was a little stronger now but not much. My friends continued not to notice it.

"We want Popsicles," the kids demanded in voices that would make dogs whimper.

"Not good for you," the potato woman said as if she'd said it before and had no hope it would do any more good this time.

I'd been on Earth long enough to know what kids are. If it came to that, kids on T'toom were not so different. They want what they want when they want it. But when the fat woman denied these kids Popsicles, one said, "No good at all," and the other said, "You're right, Auntie." Auntie looked surprised but was quick enough to take advantage of the situation. She herded the kids as she followed the android toward the beach. They let themselves be herded.

I said, "Did anything unusual happen there, or was I just not paying attention?"

"Nothing to it, dude," Whipper Will said.

The light changed again. When we still didn't cross PCH, far back in the troops, Captain Hook called, "Are we having pizza, or what?"

As we stepped into the crosswalk, I said, "Another android superpower? Making kids behave?"

"Maybe it wanna-be. Nobody knows, bro."

I noticed three more cars up the street fizzing as they evaporated. In a low voice, as if not wanting to wake the baby, Bingo said, "SA makes those too. Cars that evaporate on demand. Never again will you get snaked on a parking place. They're called Melt-O-Mobiles."

I said, "Like on the green-and-blue machines."

Whipper Will shook his head.

"No?"

"Yes. Of course. Just like. But all that SA stuff dogs me. You'll see." He shook his head again.

"I don't care who makes them," Grampa Zamp said. "They smell awful."

"You hotdogging, dude?" Whipper Will said. Zamp looked confused. "Why not?" he said.

Whatever it was that nobody else could smell, the air was full of it, thinner, then thicker, as it was pushed around by the sea breeze, but always there.

As we passed a shop a fat guy came to the front of it. In the window were T-shirts featuring spiky paintings in unnatural colors not usually seen outside a car dealer's showroom—T-shirts from Hell. Above his protruding tummy—a thick line of skin and black hair—the guy wore one of his own shirts. It did nothing for his looks. He cried, "Beautiful T-shirts! You need these beautiful T-shirts."

A crowd gathered, many people in it shouting, "I need a beautiful T-shirt!" Money and T-shirts changed hands.

I looked again. The shirts were still not beautiful. "Want a shirt?" I asked nobody in particular.

"Grotty shirts, dude," Hanger said.

Thumper nodded and said with disgust, "Dance club stuff. For gremmies and hodads only."

We skirted the crowd and came at last to Guido's, a small stucco building with a green-and-red awning that looked like a flag of the losing side in many bad battles. Along with the squat green bottles in the window was a flyspecked card that said OPEN. But we were not there for the atmosphere. For the surfers, this was the temple of pizza.

Out in front a guy in work shirt, jeans, and a Peterbilt baseball cap was counting his change. I studied the clear blue sky and experimentally said to him, "Looks like rain."

The guy looked up at the same clear blue sky and nodded as he frowned. "Funny time of year for it," he said.

The bad smell was good. It made people believe things against their own intelligence, observation, taste, and desire. I was sure that Knighten Daise would have something to say about this too. It was funny that the stuff seemed to have no effect on me and Zamp or on the surfers. Me and Zamp I could understand: We were not of this Earth. But what made the surfers in Whipper Will's house different from all the other dudes and dudettes on the beach?

After the glare outside Guido's was dark and cool and smelled of exotic spices. So little of the terrible smell was in the air, I might have only imagined it was there at all.

Our waiter was a big kid who had cannonballs for muscles. Maybe he was a Surfing Samurai Robot in a flesh-colored suit. His short hair looked like sandpaper. He glanced around the big table, appreciating the local fauns, but mostly was interested in me and Zamp. "We don't get many like you two in here," he said as if he'd said something clever.

It occurred to me that I had never been inside Guido's before. I'd eaten his pizza, but it had always been take-out, and I'd never been the one to do the taking. I said, "We're bookends. You know? Books?"

I don't know what it was, the crazy smell in the air or my sparkling personality, but he smiled as if he'd figured out addition at last, and said, "Sure. Bookends." He took our order and while we waited, Zamp rubbernecked.

Whipper Will wanted to give Bill a handful of change so he could play the video game in the corner while we ate, but Bill said, "Watch my dust." He waddled to the game, did something to it, and began to play. I had seen him do the same thing to parking meters and Laundromats.

When the kid brought the pizza, Zamp said, "This is it?"

"Give it a chance," Thumper said.

"It's very flat, isn't it?" Zamp said as he took a slice. When he bit into it his eyeballs rolled up into his head and when he was done with the first slice, he took another. Flopsie and Mopsie had a good time wiping the sauce off his face, and Zamp didn't seem to mind. By the time we left the kid was watching Bill through narrow eyes and drumming his fingers on the counter next to the cash register.

All in all the meal at Guido's was more suc-
cessful than the walk home. Whipper Will
would not look at any android, and he ignored
the clumps of people in front of the stores to
the point that he would walk right through them
as if they were clouds of insects. For him, cars
effervescing like soda water had all the fascination of cracks in the pavement. Bingo
watched him with the concern of a nurse watching a patient who had a colorful disease.

I told her, "He'll be OK."

"You don't know the whole story."

"There's a way to fix that."

She shook her head. "I can't. Whipper'll
throw it down if he gets cranked enough."

"I wouldn't want him any more cranked than
he is right now."

For some reason, Bingo looked even more
concerned after that.

The rude noises that Bill and the surfers made
at androids were sometimes mistaken for com-
ments about the owners. Not even this snapped
Whipper Will out of his trance. Bill and the
surfers worked out their problems by being as
cute and nonthreatening as a basketful of kit-
tens. We slipped past fights like a ship narrowly
missing icebergs.

When we got back to the house a woman was
reclining in the sun on a chaise lounge on the
back deck. She was relaxed enough to be asleep.
Even in repose as she was, she gave the impression of being in languid graceful motion. She
had long dark hair that fell in feathers to her

shoulders. Where the sun caught it, red coals seemed to smolder. The enormous black lenses of sunglasses covered her eyes, and from high cheekbones hung a wide mouth splashed with red, and a wicked chin. The relaxed mouth smiled a little, as if smiling came naturally to it. At the moment, she was wearing a tight, denim jumpsuit that emphasized what was most interesting about her slim body. One knee was raised a little. High boots matched her hair.

Earth women did nothing for me personally, of course, but the surfers had given me the short course in what to look for. She had all of it.

Whipper Will seemed genuinely surprised to see her. He glanced at Bingo for her reaction. Bingo's face was as emotional as a cube of butter. The woman on the chaise started suddenly, as if she had in fact been asleep, and stretched, making cats I had seen look clumsy. She said, "Hi," in the wispy voice of a child who has awakened among friends.

In a way that told me nothing, Whipper Will said, "Hello, Darken. What's shaking?"

Darken poured to her feet and hugged Whipper Will. She was just enough shorter than him to be comfortable resting her head on his shoulder. He held his hands away from her back and tried not to enjoy the hug, but his face was red when she came away. "Bingo," she said. The two women hugged, but I'd seen goldfish in a bowl be warmer.

"These are my bros," Whipper Will said, and

introduced the surfers. "Dudes, this is Darken Stormy, an old bro."

The guys leered at Darken Stormy, and the gals were reserved and suspicious. I guess it was a compliment.

"Can we talk?" said Darken. The sleep was gone from her voice now. It was as deep as the ocean and soft as a tub full of rabbits.

"Sure," said Whipper Will. "Dig my hang." He held out his hand like a waiter. Darken strolled into the house, her hips having everybody's attention. Whipper Will followed her and turned at the doorway. "You dudes want to come?"

Without saying a word Bingo slid past him into the house.

"How about you, Zoot? Zamp?"

I said, "Trust is a funny thing, isn't it?"

Whipper Will tried to smile, but his mouth was too concerned with other things to take it on. He said. "Maybe I just want witnesses."

"Fair enough." Zamp and I went into the house. I sent Bill back outside so the surfers wouldn't feel entirely abandoned.

In the living room Bingo was sitting in the middle of the couch. Across from her Darken Stormy sat in a frayed old armchair no newer than last year's wasted hours. The air was warm, but you could have ice-skated on the vibes. Whipper Will sat down next to Bingo and took her hand in his lap. It lay there like a salami. Zamp sat on a low stool and I stood behind him. From where I stood I could see through the kitchen door and out the window. The surfers were walking their surf-bots onto the back deck.

"Very groovy to see you, Darken," Whipper Will said.

"Nice to see you too."

The meaningless words floated out the open window.

"I have my own radio show now. It's on every afternoon. Perhaps you've heard it."

"No," said Bingo like a door slam.

But Zamp brightened right up. "Radio?" he said. "Like *The Shadow*? Like *Jack Benny* and *Fibber McGee*? Like *The Voice of Firestone?*" He caressed the words as he said them. Earth radio was a big deal on T'toom—it was how we knew English, but the shows were a little out of date. T'toom and Earth were far enough apart that the speed of light made historians of us all.

Darken Stormy laughed. She had a beautiful laugh, like water over stones. She said, "I'm afraid not. It's a talk show."

"A show about talking?" Zamp said.

Bingo and Whipper Will said nothing. I don't know if they were even listening. Maybe Whipper Will was just relieved that for the moment the conversation had nothing to do with him.

Darken laughed again. "We have interesting guests. People call in to talk to them."

"Eavesdropping on other people's conversations," I grumbled. But Zamp was impressed. He said, "Wow," and meant it.

Darken turned to Whipper Will and said, "You let your hair grow."

"My hair," Whipper Will said. "My brain."

She nodded and said, "Your father misses you."

Bingo and Whipper Will recoiled as if Darken Stormy had slapped them. Whipper Will said, "You still work for my father?"

"Well, for one thing," Darken Stormy said, rolling her eyes humorously, "he owns the radio station."

"And for another thing?" Whipper Will said.

"He needs you. The work on the androids is not going well."

"Bummer."

"Yes."

"I said I would never go back to Willville."

"People change their minds."

"He said no," Bingo said.

"I know what he said," Darken Stormy said.

They sounded like two lionesses fighting over a piece of meat.

Darken Stormy let her eyes wander the room. Bingo patted Whipper Will's hand, but it was just a breeze to him. Outside, Bill and the surfers were ostentatiously polishing surf-bots. Every time an android walked by on the public walkway the surfers whooped. Bill sometimes whooped too, and when he did the androids walked a little faster while casting unhappy glances over their shoulders.

Darken rose to her feet and went to the fireplace. From behind some very old flowers and some seashells and two tiny jars of colored sand she took a blue thing not much bigger than a shoe box. I had not noticed it. It looked like a lot of other junk in the surfer's house.

When Darken Stormy held it before her, I could see that it was a surfer made from pipe cleaners standing in the classic Quasimodo pose on a chip of wood that was supposed to be a surfboard. Behind the surfer a single wooden wave arched over him.

"How sweet," Darken said. "You still have it."

Bingo didn't think it was sweet. Whipper Will tried to look cool.

Darken Stormy wound a key at the back of the thing and the surfboard rocked up and back slowly to a tinkly rendition of "Surf City."

"What is it?" I said.

"A music box," Darken Stormy said. "I bought it for Whipper Will's birthday one year." She smiled again, but this one wasn't for us. It was a cozy one just for her. She said, "We had some good times, Whipper."

"We had 'em," Whipper Will said, "and they're gone, like yesterday's aggro waves. Tell Dad to stop bugging me."

"Should I tell him you're sorry you won't come back?" Darken Stormy said sarcastically.

"Tell him anything you want as long as he stops trying to snake me by sending old beddies around."

"I wanted to see you too."

"Here he is," Bingo said.

Darken Stormy held out the music box. "Can

I have this?" she said. "You don't seem to have any use for it."

At the same time, Whipper Will said "Yes" and Bingo said "No." "No," Whipper Will said.

"I see." More carefully than I would have expected, she set it back onto the mantel. She turned and ran her hands down her hips. I think if I'd been a human male the top of my head would have come off at that point. She said, "You'll be hearing from him."

"Groovy," said Whipper Will as if it were no such thing.

Using that special hip motion that only human females can manage she strolled past the couch to me and Zamp. From a breast pocket she pulled a business card and bent over to give it to Zamp, thus giving Whipper Will a really astonishing view of her ass. It was one of the most difficult things he'd ever done, but Whipper Will didn't look. Or maybe he did. He might have been good enough.

To Gramp Zamp, Darken Stormy said, "You're kind of cute. Call my talk show anytime. We'll talk." The way she said it, talking should have been illegal without a marriage license. She walked out of the room, through the kitchen, and out the back door. She watched Bill and the surfers for a moment before she went away.

The surfers missed the show. They were too involved with insulting androids to notice. "Ahh-roooh!" they cried.

3

Iron Will

Bingo was still sitting on the couch. Whipper Will was standing in the middle of the room raking his hair with his hand. Grampa Zamp was sniffing the card. When he saw me, he said, "This is great. In about forty years, I'll be a radio star on T'toom."

I nodded but I had things on my mind other than Grampa Zamp's stardom. Darken Stormy had shaken up Whipper Will and probably done worse than that to Bingo, but she still hadn't done anything illegal. She'd only mentioned androids in a way that caused me to believe that Whipper Will had more than a casual connection with them. That interested me. I wasn't yet working for Knighten Daise and already androids interested me.

I sat down on one end of the couch. Bingo attempted to smile at me, but it was a weak thing with a lot of worry in it. For a moment I listened to Bill and the surfers whooping on the back deck. Then I said, "Does Darken Stormy come with instructions or should I just guess?"

"She's just an old girlfriend," Whipper Will said as if he were reading baseball scores.

Bingo said, "Hang loose, dude. I'm not dissed by her."

Certainly no more than by a broken foot, I thought. I said, "She's an old girlfriend. What made you break up?" I was just a nosy old friend of the family. Whipper Will could have asked me why it was my business and that would have been the end of it, but I could see he wanted to talk.

He waited for Bingo to speak. When she didn't, he said, "I used to work at the Superhero Android labs. Darken was a model at Will Industries trade shows. We met out at Willville, and . . ." He tried to jack up his voice with his hands.

Bingo said. "As you can see, she's quite a dish."

"You're not exactly chopped sushi yourself," Whipper Will said.

"Go on," Bingo said, not buying any soft soap right now.

"She *is* quite a dish," Whipper Will said as if he were admitting he'd killed Cock Robin. "And I was the boss man's son and we got pretty stoked on each other. But she was cranked on BMWs and Rolexes and the old white picket fence. She guzzled the right brewski and draped the fresh threads. We sizzled and slashed top-to-bottom for a while but the wipeout came hard and we were both dogged bad."

"Raw," said Bingo, and she shook her head. She did not sound sorry.

Not very kindly, I said, "And now she's shilling for your father."

"A grotty scene," Whipper Will said.

I expected Bingo to say, "Grotty," but she didn't. A sound outside the front of the house saved her the trouble. If a pride of lions had suddenly materialized on Whipper Will's front porch and some brave soul had stroked them ever so gently under their chins, they might have made a sound like this. The four of us went to see what it was.

Parked across the front of Whipper Will's garage was the biggest, blackest car I had ever seen. Its color was the deep emptiness of outer space and you could launch aircraft from its roof. The engine stopped—stopping the lions—and a man in a chauffeur's uniform got out. He wasn't wearing a tie but a blue plastic collar that complemented his beauty. He walked back about a block and pulled open a door.

The man who climbed out looked the way Whipper Will might look in about thirty years if he cut his hair and changed his tailor. The suit he wore was dark but not black, an indefinable color that spoke of vaults with the lights off but full of money. The suit fit him perfectly. It had fewer wrinkles than a china plate. The man walked toward us smiling.

"Whipper, my boy," the man cried as he held out his hand.

"Hello, Dad," Whipper Will said, and shook his hand without enthusiasm.

"Miss Binghamton," Whipper Will's dad said, and tried to shake hands with Bingo. She wasn't having any. After a while he put his hand down, reminding me of Bill.

Whipper Will's dad looked at us, expecting somebody to throw him a fish, but Whipper Will didn't say or do anything. He just waited, listening to the traffic go by. A boxy car that might once have been green pulled into a parking space in the lot of the liquor store across the street. Instead of getting out and going into the store the driver pulled out a newspaper and held it a little too low. Even from here I could see his eyes. Searching, curious eyes.

"May I come in?" Whipper Will's dad said.

"Sure, dude," Whipper Will said, and his dad winced, not liking the word *dude* much.

Everybody but the chauffeur went inside. Whipper Will's father sat at one end of the couch and said, "Sit down, sit down," as if it were his house. Whipper Will sat on the arm at the other end of the couch. Bingo sat where Darken Stormy had been sitting before. I stood at the entrance to the hallway and held up the wall. Zamp was just behind me.

Coldly, Whipper Will said, "Dudes, this is my dad, Iron Will. He got here so fast he must have been waiting for Darken Stormy around the corner. He probably guessed I wouldn't get stoked on her rap."

"I know you can speak English," Mr. Will said. "I paid enough for your education."

"Right on," Whipper Will said, and smiled.

"Why won't you come back?" Mr. Will said.

"It's not you, Dad. It's not even the androids. It's the whole big business whoopie. Fancy clothes, meetings, deadlines, office politics. I came to the beach to hang loose, to cruise without any of it."

Calmly, as if explaining playground etiquette to a small child, Mr. Will said, "I don't suppose it means anything to you that SA and Will Industries need you. It took us long enough to finish developing a commercial android after you left. But the current series gets moldy and hard. It crumbles away just like bread. You can help us design one that won't go stale. I'd make it worth your while. You could have anything you wanted."

"Really?" said Whipper Will with sudden interest.

"Anything."

"The one thing I want," Whipper Will said, his words suddenly growing hair and teeth, "is for you to leave me alone."

I sympathized with Whipper Will. I had barely escaped the family business myself.

Mr. Will said, "What do you say, Miss Binghamton? You used to be his assistant. I could make it worth *your* while too."

Bingo looked away. The curtains swaying in the breeze were not as interesting as she made them.

I could see where the conversation was going. Bingo and Whipper and his father could circle each other like that all afternoon. They were starting in on each other again when I walked back down the hallway and went out the front door. I suggested Zamp speak with the chauffeur. While Zamp went over to look in the limousine's window, I went across the street to look in a window of my own.

I walked past the liquor store and then came back across the lot. While I did that, a very groovy teenage dude and dudette approached a Melt-O-Mobile machine that stood just outside the liquor store's front door. As if he were buying diamonds for her but doing nothing at all compared to what he *could* do if he put his mind to it, the dude shoved a few bills into the machine. It groaned and something as tall as the slit and as wide as a hand grew slowly from it. When it was outside the machine, the thick sheet suddenly snapped open and became a Melt-O-Mobile that bounced a little as it settled on the blacktop. The two groovy types got into it and the dude drove them away.

Even knowing that Melt-O-Mobiles would not be very popular if they stranded a person wherever he or she went, actually seeing a dispenser perform was a surprise. It was the difference between hearing about an elephant and seeing one. I almost got run over while I stood there being astonished.

But a loud honk from a guy in a passing Datsun snapped me out of my daze. From behind I

approached the green car that had followed the
Will limousine, watching the guy's face in the side
mirror, which meant that he could see me. His
eyes flickered but otherwise he didn't move. He
didn't even turn the page of his newspaper.

I stood next to his open window and said,
"He'll be inside for a while. He and his son are
having a little party."

"I don't know what you're talking about."

"No. That's why you're sitting over here not
reading yesterday's paper." I looked in at him.
I was the right height to do it without bending.
He must have been tall because the black brush
of his hair tickled the ceiling of the car. He had
the wide-open face of an extra in a Gino and
Darlene flick, with a polka-dot bow tie stationed
below it. His dark blue suit was tasteful enough
to be rented. I had seen him before.

He said, "So far, sitting in a car is not a
crime."

"We almost met at Kilroy's. You were another one of the detectives who'd been invited
to help the Hawaiian UFO Aliens solve their
problem."

Very slowly, he turned his head to look at me.
He smiled in a way that managed not to mean
anything and said, "You may be a pro, but
you're not from around here."

"Bay City," I said.

He laughed and caught it before it escaped.
He stuck his hand out through the window and
said, "Irv Doewanit."

"Zoot Marlowe," I said, and shook his hand.

"Marlowe, eh?" He liked it a lot.

I took a chance and said, "You following Mr. Will?"

"If you're half the pro you pretend to be you know I can't tell you that."

"I know," I said. "I just wanted to make sure that *you* know. We should talk."

"I can't talk—"

"Not about your client or your job. Just talk. One gumshoe to another."

"Shop talk. It's been a while."

"You have your own shop?"

"In a manner of speaking."

He gave me a Hollywood address up on Ivar and we agreed to meet that evening. I ran back across PCH feeling noble as a statue in a park but more lively. Doewanit was a real detective. We would talk. Oh yes, we would.

When I got to Whipper's house a Melt-O-Mobile was pulling up. The driver got out, and I could see by the blue plastic collar that it was an android. Superhero Android. He went to the front door and knocked. He glanced at me when I walked up but said nothing. We waited for the answer together.

Bingo opened the door. She looked tired. Behind her, Whipper and his father were shouting at each other. They stopped when Bingo and the android and I walked into the living room. Mr. Will smiled and said, "At last. Get your friends together, Whipper. We're going for a ride."

"Where?" said Whipper as if he didn't much care.

"Nowhere special. I just want to show off the Melt-O-Mobile."

Whipper said something about Melt-O-Mobiles that was rude and anatomically impossible. Mr. Will began to burn. Personally, I was getting tired of watching them push each other off their soapboxes. I said, "A ride couldn't hurt. And the dudes would get cranked on it."

I watched Whipper calculating what was in it for him, for his friends, for his father. His father just smiled as he rubbed his hands together. Not very happy, but fortified with steel plate, Whipper said, "Groovy."

Mr. Will and his android took Thumper and Flopsie and Mopsie for a ride. While they were gone, Bingo and Whipper stood in front of the the front door swaying as they hugged. The smell that made people believe stuff hung in the air like a bad idea. The surfers whooped at androids and sang snatches of songs they'd learned from Gino and Darlene.

When the Melt-O-Mobile came back Thumper leapt from it and cried, "That android is one aggro dude! He drives like the gnarly kahuna himself! Bitchen dude. Bitchen dude." He shook his head in wonder.

"Driving well in traffic is his superpower," Mr. Will said as he helped Flopsie and Mopsie from the car. They were charmed at the attention, and each did her best to act like the Queen of England. Mr. Will called, "Next!"

Whipper refused to go and Bingo wouldn't even discuss it. I looked at Whipper. No point working at making him an enemy. He nodded. I rode out with Bill, Mr. Will, the android, and the rest of the surfers.

The ride was pretty much what you'd expect to have in a cardboard car. We bumped along feeling every crack in the street. The air and traffic noise were so loud I felt as if I were riding on a skateboard. But the android was as good a driver as Thumper had said. He weaved in and out between cars with all the effort of Rubinstein playing a Mozart sonata. I'd seen guys sweat more at stoplights.

While we made the rounds I saw more people vend themselves Melt-O-Mobiles. I didn't gawk the way I had the first time, but watching didn't bore me either.

We got back, and Mr. Will did his big finish. After the driving android got into the limousine Mr. Will reached into the Melt-O-Mobile and pushed a button on the dash that started the roof of the car fizzing. While the car ate itself the bad smell grew stronger. As casually as a striking rattlesnake, Mr. Will said, "You know, Whipper, you'd enjoy working for me again."

Whipper and Bingo looked at him as if he were crazy. I knew he wasn't crazy. I watched him as if he were doing card tricks.

"Don't you think?" Mr. Will said.

"One of us is thinking," Whipper said, "and it isn't you."

Mr. Will frowned. While he did that, a tall blond woman wearing cutoff jeans and a red halter top swayed by. Captain Hook, always handy with the ladies, shouted at her, "I'm good for you, baby!" and made a kissing noise.

The blonde looked a little confused, but instead of continuing her one-woman parade she swayed over to Captain Hook and said, "You're good for me, baby." She wrapped her hands around his neck.

The other surfers howled, "Ahh-roooh!" and even Captain Hook looked surprised. But he said, "Come on in. We'll down a brewski and rap." Holding her hand, Captain Hook towed her inside as if she were a boat made of glass.

I said, "Interesting, isn't it?"

"What?" Mr. Will said.

"Cars start evaporating and people will believe anything."

"What are you implying?"

"Nothing much," I said. "But a sort of 'credulity' gas must be good for business."

"I don't know what *your* business is, Mr. Marlowe, but I suspect you're not a chemist. If this 'credulity' gas is in the air it must be something new in the smog. Besides"—he looked sideways at Whipper—"not everybody seems to believe everything." That bothered him, and he thought about it.

Whipper thought about it too. It was amazing how much he and his father looked alike when they both had their faces twisted up like that.

Bingo said, "It doesn't matter. Whipper isn't going back to work for you."

"Is that so?" Mr. Will said, his voice taking on an edge sharp enough to remove flesh. "I'm not making threats, but sometimes coincidences happen. You do something bad to me—it just could be that something bad will happen to your no-account friends."

Whipper said, "It just could be you're full of shit."

Mr. Will didn't wait for his chauffeur to let him back into the limousine. He got in and slammed the door harder than he had to. The lions began to purr again and the limousine swung out into the street as if there were no traffic to watch for.

Whipper laughed and shook his head. "Oh, Dad. I can't take him anywhere."

"That sounded like a threat to me," I said as I watched Irv Doewanit pull into traffic and follow the limousine.

"Dad's tough, and he's a little ruthless in business, but he wouldn't actually hurt anybody."

Whipper and Bingo and the surfers went back into the house. I took a lot of time staring at the place where I'd last seen Doewanit's green car and the limousine.

Zamp said, "You think Whipper's wrong about his dad?"

"It would be safer to think so."

Bill said, "I can think so for you."

"You do that," I said. "Though I have the feeling I won't need the help."

4
Nuts from Hollywood

Zamp and Bill and I were still standing outside Whipper's house when Captain Hook's blonde stormed out of the place. She didn't stop to speak to us, but her angry face told us enough. A moment later, Captain Hook came to the door with a red handprint on one cheek. He cried, "Tisha!" but the blonde was long gone and her sonic boom with her.

"I been snaked!" Captain Hook said.

"I guess that was her problem too," I said, and went into the house with my entourage. Zamp asked me what the time was. When I told him he got excited and jabbered that Darken Stormy's radio program would be on any minute. He took the card from the pocket of his Hawaiian shirt and asked me to dial the number for him.

"Ask Whipper to teach you how to read," I said as I dialed. "Except for being thrown out of his house and avoiding his father, I don't think he's very busy."

Zamp sat down with the phone and he spoke to somebody who passed him on to somebody else. At last he put his hand over the receiver and said, "I'm on hold. Darken will be with me in a moment."

"Congratulations."

The TV had a radio in it and I switched it on. I tuned away from the oldies station it habitually played and, after crossing through static and garbage, heard Darken Stormy say, ". . . a surprise guest. A mysterious gentleman known to me only as Grampa Zamp. He'll be telling us a little about himself. Stay tuned." A commercial started. It suggested in ways that were not very subtle that some hospital in Orange County could help me lose weight while eating everything on the menu and never leaving the couch. I guess if you need to lose weight, that's the way to do it.

Darken Stormy came back and introduced Grampa Zamp again, and then she was interviewing him. He answered into the telephone and five seconds later his voice came from the radio. When Zamp seemed confused by the way things were going, Darken told him the show was on a five-second tape delay and suggested he turn down his radio. He gestured at me frantically and I swung closed the door between kitchen, where Zamp was, and the living room, where the radio was. By that time the show had attracted Captain Hook and the other surfers. "Yes," Zamp said, "I'm a noted futurist from a planet called T'toom."

I looked at the kitchen door, shocked as if . . . well, shocked as if Zamp had admitted he was from another planet. Whipper and Bingo looked at me with their eyebrows up. They'd suspected for a long time that my story about being from Bay City was just a story. Anybody with half a brain would, if they cared. Most people didn't care or were afraid to get involved in something that might be too big or too unpleasant for them. After all, Orson Welles hadn't been the last person to suggest that invading the Earth was a good idea.

The other surfers laughed and poked each other in the ribs as Zamp spoke about abo trees and sap and household ooze and slaberingeo spines. Sunday supplement stuff on T'toom, but it would be hot news on Earth if anybody believed you. Evidently, most of the surfers thought Zamp's rap was a joke. Darken Stormy was treating it that way too. Zamp telling the truth to Darken Stormy and to her audience was no more dangerous than my telling the truth to a crystal-bending swami like Goneout Backson.

I relaxed, and instead of listening to Grampa Zamp I thought about androids and Melt-O-Mobiles and credulity gas. They just drifted through my mind with no more weight or importance than clouds. I didn't know enough about anything. Besides, none of this was my business yet, though it probably would be if Mr. Daise hired me. He said he had android trouble.

I had trouble too, but it had nothing to do with androids. A certain guy who owned a certain house was about to eject certain occupants onto PCH like spent bullets. I worked the problem over in my head with a sap and a rubber hose and with bamboo shoots under the fingernails. What Max Toodemax was pulling wasn't nice, but as far as I could tell it was legal. As legal as selling painless weight-loss plans to people whose exercise of choice was thumbing the remote control on their TV.

Cheering and applause yanked me back from the land where half-bright detectives go to think. The kitchen door was open and Zamp's nose was quivering happily. He said, "For being on her show today, Darken is sending me two free tickets to the upcoming Will Industries Trade Show."

"Groovy," Whipper said without inflection.

"You'll go with me, won't you Zoot?"

"Sure. Me and whose army?"

"You won't need an army," Whipper said, and laughed.

"I guess you're right. Your dad doesn't want me or Zamp."

Whipper was angry at me. It was buried, but not very deep. He really did like his father. "Chill out, dude," he said.

"If I don't bring an army, is it OK if I'm careful?" I said.

Whipper shrugged and left the room.

Whipper spent the afternoon teaching Zamp to read. When I came into the kitchen to kibitz, Whipper said, "I guess we both got too cranked."

"Sure. Being cranked is the curse of the thinking class."

"Yeah," he answered as if I'd said something smart. "Being careful can't hurt."

We were fine after that. I still wished I had an army, and he still thought I was overreacting, but each let the other have his silly notions.

The Sun went down, turning the clouds to colors that lipstick manufacturers only dream about. When the Sun was just a shimmering fluorescent dome at the edge of the world, Bill and I walked through the yard where Whipper grew natural ingredients to put into his yoyogurt and, occasionally, flowers. On the other side was the garage.

Inside, the dim garage smelled of dust and tiny wild creatures. By the light of the single bare bulb my 1960 Chevrolet Belvedere glowed like an egg under murky water. Whipper had evidently taken care of it while I'd been gone. It was clean and full of gas. I opened the garage door and let in the yellow evening; the stores along PCH were lit like a stage set. Cars blew by on the cool ocean wind, casual as kids on skateboards.

I let Bill into the Belvedere and then myself. The doors made a solid sound when they closed and I hoped it was a good omen. The steering wheel felt solid too. I gave Irv Doewanit's address to Bill and he said, "I got it, Boss." I backed carefully onto PCH and roared along the coast toward Los Angeles and the Santa Monica Freeway. It was as if I'd never left town.

The ocean looked like beaten bronze in a forge. As the Sun went down, the fire died until the ocean was gray, and then it was just a big wild presence to my right, smelling of salt and rotting kelp and manly romance.

I turned inland on the Santa Monica Freeway and boomed through the westside among ordinary cars and Melt-O-Mobiles. The occasional android driver weaved in and out of traffic, exercising his superpower. Either that, or more or less normal Earth people still drove like idiots.

At Bill's direction, I went north on La Brea past gas stations and small businesses that may have been fronts for things more profitable. This was not quite the bad part of town but it had potential. At Olympic I crossed over to Highland and continued up, wondering when the city would decide that the beautiful palm trees between the north and southbound lanes were taking up too much space to be worthwhile.

Suddenly Hollywood slapped me in the face. Despite the mayor's attempts to clean it up so it would look like the old movies, Hollywood was still bright and garish enough to be a Christmas tree ornament designed by a seven-year-old. Homeless people would still shuffle over the stars on the Walk of Fame, indistinguishable from the stuff they pushed in shopping carts. If the real planet Earth was in any way similar to the pest hole I'd described on

T'toom, it was because of this sorry kind of thing.

I drove along Sunset ignoring the neon so I could watch the traffic. Neon always excited Bill, and he could hardly stay still in his seat. Maybe it was the electricity. We passed the Crossroads of the World, a quaint thirties idea of international architecture, and came to Ivar.

"One block up," Bill said. Turning left was not a treat, but I managed it after waiting three lights. The business day was over and it was too early for the movie crowd, so I actually found a place to park on the street. I didn't even have to put money into the meter.

"Where?" I said.

Bill pointed to a building like a lot of others on the street. The bottom floor was a long arcade of bright fluorescent light that made food look poisonous and made the postcards of local attractions look repulsive. Bill couldn't get enough of it. Above the souvenir shops was the somber gray front of a cheap office building. I nodded. This was just the kind of neighborhood where I would expect to find a shamus like Irv Doewanit.

I crossed the street and passed a number of dark foreign-looking men, each of whom stood in the doorway of a store, each store selling exactly the same merchandise. For only slightly less than they were paying for a night's lodging, out-of-towners could buy anything they wanted as long as it said HELLO FROM HOLLYWOOD on it or portrayed their favorite star—something to show the folks back home they'd actually been here. Back home, in the telling, Hollywood would acquire a polish it hadn't had for years.

"Come on, Bill," I said, and yanked him away from a spinner of garish postcards.

Bill and I passed a man who had a suspicious face. He tried a lightning smile as we passed, but when we turned into the narrow stairway between his store and the next one the smile flared out like the flame of a match.

Light and sound faded as we climbed. At the top was a long hallway as narrow as the stairs. It was lit by good intentions as much as by the small electric sconces in the walls that were the height of fashion even before Philip Marlowe came to town. They had been cleaner then. Quiet was a thick dusty curtain.

I stood at the top of the staircase peering along the shabby hallway, knowing it probably looked worse in the daytime when you could see the cracks in the walls, the peeling paint that had once been a color, the dust and cobwebs in the corners. Maybe there was graffiti too, just for spice. The smell was of old age, death, and constant human habitation. I looked back down the stairs. The suspicious man looked up at me, saw I was looking down, and stepped out of sight.

"Is this the right place?" I said.

Bill read me back the right address. I stepped quietly along the hall, trying not to disturb the worn carpet, looking for Irv Doewanit's name on a pebbled door. Bill bobbed beside me. I said, "Let's have some light."

"Right, Boss." Light snapped out of Bill's eyes in twin yellow cones. It did nothing to improve the decor, but finding Doewanit's office became easier. I had passed it and now I went back, walking softly by the chiropractors, employment agencies, and coin dealers, so as not to awaken them.

Yellow light was behind the glass. I knocked. Footsteps danced across the floor, and the door opened wide enough to admit several flies. It then opened wider. Doewanit smiled and said, "Marlowe, Marlowe." He let me and Bill into his office.

5

The Perfect Place

Irv Doewanit's office was a small sickly box coated with flaking green paint. Mud had more style. A filing cabinet, not too badly battered, stood in the corner under a potted cactus. Over the cactus hung a calendar showing a photograph of a very slick automobile with a lot of fins and chrome. Another door led somewhere, maybe to a closet. The rush of traffic came in through a window open just wide enough to let in some air.

Even after my two previous trips to Earth I hadn't let myself hope that there was a place this perfect. If Philip Marlowe existed in any flesh at all I would come no closer than Irv Doewanit. "This is the place, Bill," I said, just enjoying being in this terrible room.

"The street, the building, the address," Bill said proudly.

With a grunt, Doewanit sat down at a desk as old as God's desk. He was not so perfect, at least as far as private eyes went. He still wore a polka-dot bow tie and a dark blue suit. He looked happy and healthy. Sitting there, he looked like a flower in a gravel pit.

Doewanit motioned to the client's chair, which waited patiently, like an old horse. I sat down and rested my elbows on the battered arms. Bill stood beside me. He looked at me, shining light into my eyes. I told him we'd had enough and his eyelights went away.

Doewanit pulled a brown bottle from a drawer and said, "Drink?"

"Sure," I said. "In a dirty glass. With a hair in it."

Doewanit laughed and said, "You know, some guys might think patter like that was a little overripe."

He was right, of course. I was just nervous to be talking to a real human detective. I fought down my jitters as he put two clean glasses on the blotter and filled each of them halfway. While he did this he said, "Marlowe, Marlowe, you're no more from Bay City than I am."

"Where am I from?"

He appraised me the way he would a hot watch. "Please don't play those games with me. If I knew where you were from I wouldn't ask, would I?"

I sipped my drink. It was stronger than my normal brewski and burned on the way down. I took another sip and my brain began to float free and easy. I said, "We lived too close to the nuclear power plant. You should see my brother. He has ears like an elephant." Living dangerously, I said, "You'd probably like my sister."

He laughed again and shook his head, not believing a word of it.

I said, "I seem to be doing all the talking."

Doewanit apparently thought so too. He pointed at me and said, "I'm a detective. For fifty bucks a day I'll sit outside anybody's house in my car. For a hundred bucks a day I'll even watch who goes in and out."

Bill laughed at that, looked at me, and stopped.

"Sure," I said. "The rates are printed on the back of the license. Somehow you don't seem the type."

"Please," he said, and tossed back most of his drink. He was good. Smoke did not come out of his ears. "Looks aren't everything. And, unlike Philip Marlowe, I sometimes even take divorce business. I have to. Job one is survival."

I glanced around the office and said, "Job two can't be interior decoration."

"No," he said, not pleased to be agreeing with me. "I've come a long way since I was a staff writer for *Charlie Sundown*."

"On TV?" I said. Charlie Sundown was a detective who had more charm than brains. The bad guys beat him up three or four times in the course of an episode, but they never broke anything important. He was a handsome hunk who always got the girl and always cracked the case. He never ran out of gas or bullets. His show was a favorite of the surfers.

Bill started to sing the theme song in clear electronic tones. I would have stopped him, but Doewanit seemed to enjoy it. One finger conducted. When Bill started again Doewanit asked him to stop. Bill stopped in midnote and Doewanit said, "I got tired of just talking the talk and decided to try walking the walk. I guess I believed my own lies about detectives."

I nodded, knowing what lies he meant. I watched *Charlie Sundown* too, in spite of myself.

He told me *Charlie Sundown* stories that made me wonder who had a hard enough head to take that much abuse. And that was just the writers. When the first brown bottle was empty Doewanit pulled a full one from his drawer.

It got a little drunk out. The brewski tasted good; it warmed on its way down instead of burning and made a comfy sun in my tummy. The cheap room retreated and Doewanit's face seemed to grow and glow a little, as if a light bulb were behind it. Traffic noise whispered secrets to the street. Only the smell of dust and of human decay seemed to get stronger. I had trouble sitting up straight in my chair. Bill propped me up on one side. Androids and Whipper's problem with his dad and sudden eviction and Knighten Daise continued to squirrel around in the back of my mind.

I carefully set my glass on the desk and said, not very neatly, "You were tailing Mr. Will." A complete sentence. Pretty good.

"What of it? I tail a lot of people. Sometimes

all at once." He giggled at that like a dripping faucet.

"For who? For why? For how? For huh?" The part of my mind not up to its chin in brewski knew I was not expressing myself in the clearest possible terms. "For huh?" I said again, just to confirm how little sense I was making.

He leaned toward me across the desk, carefully set his elbows in place, and rested his head in his hands. He said, "Those Wills are crazy. All of them. Not just Iron and Whipper, but Trespassers, Last, and Testa. All of them." For emphasis he flung one hand aside and nearly knocked over the bottle. "All of them," he grumbled to himself, and I thought he'd fallen asleep.

I knew Doewanit was right, of course, even from dealing with Whipper Will. The fact that a guy like Whipper, with an education and a brain to use it, lived at the beach with a troupe of gazabos made him a little eccentric in his taste, if not exactly crazed. Mr. Will didn't seem nuts so much as driven. Which made him nuts, of course.

Which didn't prove anything. Earth people in general were nuts. I'd come back to Earth for a third time. Out loud, I said, "I guess that makes me nuts too."

Doewanit spoke to his desk. He sounded as if he were crying when he said, "Not us, Marlowe. We're just two swell guys, all ready for the prom."

"Sure. We'll need a prom. Neither of us in any condition to drive."

Bill chuckled, but Doewanit laughed at that for a few hours. His mind couldn't get traction on a thought. By the time he stopped laughing we'd both forgotten why he'd started, so he sang me a song. Then I sang him one and then we sang together. We sang a lot. Then we told stories and threatened each other and made up and pledged eternal brotherhood. I may have told him where I was really from. I don't suppose it mattered anyway; he wouldn't have noticed if I'd tattooed it on his chest.

Far away, a ghost was shrieking at me and shattering my brain with the big hammer of its voice. The tornado that twisted from my stomach up into my head was stirring the shattered bits. My nose throbbed, throwing waves of sickness into the rest of my body. And that ghost was still shrieking. The bits made patterns of androids and melting cars and credulity gas. They wanted to make sense but I couldn't help them. I was busy listening to that shrieking.

Little by little I was glad to notice that the shrieking was not inside my head but outside. I opened my eyes and saw something very close that was shiny and brown. The shrieking was a siren. Something went by on Sunset and incidentally shattered my brains. Somebody's tax dollars at work.

Carefully, I sat up. The shiny brown thing was the edge of Irv Doewanit's desk. Doewanit himself sat across from me with his head down. I'd have been a little disappointed if he did not feel as terrible as I did. My nose looked normal but from the inside it felt as if somebody were trying to slug his way out with his fists. Good rhythmic slugging too.

Sunlight came through the blinds and made stripes against the walls and floor. Traffic passed outside. In the next office a typewriter and a radio were going. The world was up and busy. I shuddered.

"OK, Boss?" Bill said.

"I hope not. I wouldn't want to feel this terrible and still be OK." My thoughts moved like goldfish, first making sensible patterns and then not. As slowly as they moved, they were too quick for me.

Doewanit lifted his head as if he were lifting a bowling ball at the end of a soda straw. He squinted at the light and gingerly ran a hand through his hair. Sacks hung under his eyes. Bursts of red blotched his face. He smacked his lips and sucked his teeth like an old man. He grunted.

I grunted just to hold up my end. There was something about the credulity gas, a connection I'd missed. I'd seen it recently in the fish tank of my mind, and I just about had the facts lined up again when I sneezed. The sneeze was big and explosive, making Doewanit draw back from me.

My nose no longer throbbed and my head was clear. I felt as fresh as a Beverly Hills lawn after a spring shower, but my comfort hadn't improved the looks of the office. Doewanit's face still looked as if it had been drawn on a burlap bag. The fish tank was gone and with it my bright idea. If I had not been imagining it all along.

I smiled at Doewanit and he moaned. I said, "Sneezing cures hangovers."

"The first I hear of it."

"Cured mine."

He looked at me sideways, then felt around in his desk and came up with a tissue. He took a big breath and blew hard. Looking very pale, he ran for the second door, got it open, and slammed it shut. He made disgusting noises into water. I walked to the window and looked down onto Sunset. Traffic flowed by smoothly. Tourists gawked. The smog was not life threatening. It was a beautiful day.

The door to the bathroom opened and I turned around. Doewanit leaned against the jamb, looking a little better, but still not happy. He said, "Bay City. Hah!"

I said, "Not all my ideas are good. Some of them aren't even smart. Sorry."

He nodded as if he didn't want to nod. He shook hands with me and with Bill, and the two of us went out down the ancient hallway. Insect noises of small purposeless activity came from behind some of the doors. Some of the offices were as dead as they had been the night before. Downstairs, the light was more natural but the same dark men were selling the same gaudy merchandise.

In the car, I said, "Knighten Daise. You remember the address?"

Bill tapped the side of his head and said, "The old bubble memory."

I drove west and up a few blocks to Franklin.

6

Knighten Daise
of the Foreign Legion

The last time I'd been to the Daise mansion, Mr. Daise and his daughter Heavenly had been haranguing each other about the family business. It took a lot of haranguing, I guess, because the business was Surfing Samurai Robots, the biggest producer of robots in the world. Bill was an SSR, one of the smaller, cheaper models, without the rippling muscles and the prerecorded personality.

That last time Mr. Daise looked like a lobster. He'd done this to himself in an attempt to fool industrial spies and other enemies. I don't know if being a lobster had made him safer, but it allowed him to hiss in a strange nerveracking voice that made him sound as if he were trying to haunt a house.

The houses on Franklin still looked like Greek temples or as if they should have had forty acres of cotton growing out back. The Daise mansion stood out from these pieces of stone fantasy like a tractor among racing cars. It was a square gray building that had the look of a penitentiary. Mr. Daise liked his security and he didn't care who knew it.

At the bottom of the long sweeping drive I spoke into a squawk box and a quiet cultured voice answered—the voice of Davenport, the Daise's robotler. The gate swung open and I drove through a wide grassy field full of trees I knew were fake. Each tree was a sentry box from which an armed robot guard kept watch. If they hadn't been expecting me Davenport could have hosed off my remains after he picked up what he could in a teaspoon. At the top of the drive was a big shiny car that was brown the way sunsets are orange. Next to it my Belvedere looked like a lump of tinfoil.

One half of the double front doors opened and Davenport stepped out to watch us. He was a little taller than the average human and was almost the same fancy shade of brown as the car. He wore fawn gray pants and a soft, white shirt that was open at the throat. Around his forehead was the samurai headband that meant he was not just any robot but a high-end Surfing Samurai Robot. Bill seemed to be in awe of him. He took no notice of Bill whatsoever.

He bowed ever so slightly from the waist and intoned, "It's good to see you again, Mr. Marlowe."

"The same way it's good to see a plumber when you're up to your ankles in water?"

Davenport tried to be amused by that, but his designers hadn't quite gotten the cynical smile just right. Bill's laughter was gaudy, but it sounded a lot more natural. Davenport said, "Of course," and showed me into the mansion.

The foyer was two stories high and made from wood that looked as if it had come from very old, very fine violins. There were the same fanciful tapestries, the same spectacular rose windows, the same stiff chairs that encouraged you to think you were better off standing.

Davenport left me in the library. Three walls were bookshelves. The fourth was tall windows that let in a lot of very quiet, yellow light. A leather couch stood halfway across the room and facing the desk. But maybe it wasn't a library at all. Maybe the room was just some new kind of stable.

The flat, thick reek of the animal was not quite strong enough to knock off my hat. The animal itself stood behind the desk and it was the size of a horse, but with a hump like the Paramount Pictures mountain. Its fur was an unfortunate shade of brown, much like the color of the carpet in the hallway outside Irv Doewanit's office. A big plastic tray of grass sat on the desk. The animal chewed without hurry while it studied me with its empty brown eyes, two big globs of not-very-clean motor oil. It was a camel—I'd seen them in Foreign Legion movies. It was even wearing a Foreign Legion cap, a handkerchief draped from the cap down the back of its head.

I looked around wondering if I was in the wrong room.

"Yikes!" Bill shouted, and walked toward the camel. "Pretty horsie," he said. "Pretty horsie."

In a voice as thick and flat as the smell it gave off, the camel said, "We'll have to upgrade our software if your bot thinks I'm a horse."

As far as I knew, camels didn't talk. Of course, lobsters don't talk either. I put my hands into my trench-coat pockets and said, "Good morning, Mr. Daise."

"You took your time getting here."

I smiled. Mr. Daise would reach his point eventually.

Mr. Daise said, "Sit down."

I kept standing. I said, "I guess after a while being a lobster loses its charm."

Mr. Daise swallowed, and a large lump moved down his throat. He tore off more grass and said around it, "My enemies are everywhere. I would not be so foolish as to believe that they are stupid. Eventually they would discover my ruse. It was necessary for me to change disguises."

I said, "You certainly have a talent for it. Bill, get away from there. Sit down."

Bill had been plucking at the grass in the tray with one hand. Now he came back to sit on the leather couch. While Mr. Daise continued to chew, I said, "Why are you having Iron Will followed?"

"Is somebody following him? What makes you think it's me?"

"Trouble is my business."

Mr. Daise spit into a large golden jug that rang like a gong when it was hit. He said, "I tried to contact you. But you were obviously not available. You can't expect me to wait on a thing like this."

"I don't expect anything from you, Mr. Daise. You are a constant surprise to me. You have a good chance to surprise me again by telling me why you called."

Mr. Daise stopped chewing for a moment. He swallowed and said, "Irv Doewanit is a good boy, but he lacks experience. That's why I need you."

I nodded, promising nothing.

"I'm not afraid of competition," said the camel who was Mr. Daise. "I thrive on it. I'd stack SSR robots against anybody's in a fair test." He rhapsodized on that theme for a while, bursting with fire and passion—if fire and passion is a quality camels can have. "And so," he went on, "I am more than a little offended when somebody like Iron Will puts out products like those cheeseball androids and those cardboard cars."

He didn't need me to nod, but I did anyway.

"They are garbage, pure and simple. The androids crumble to dust in a few weeks and if you're in a traffic accident in one of those Melt-O-Mobiles you don't even have time to say good-bye."

"Why are they so popular?"

"Why is anything popular? It's new. It's developed a cult following for who knows what reason. And then . . ." Mr. Daise said, his eyebrows up. He almost managed to make his camel face look cynical. Or maybe I just imagined it. "And then, there's the matter of the credulity gas."

I nodded again.

"You know about it?"

"I've seen it work. Mr. Will says it's something new in the smog."

Mr. Daise made a long camel bray. Several books withered and fell to the floor. Or maybe I was just imagining things again. "The smog," he said sarcastically. "If you believe that, you're not half the detective I want to hire. As a matter of fact I *know* it's not the smog. I have an operative researching it already."

"Then you don't need me."

"Don't get huffy. My operative is Carla De-Wilde. She's an SSR I donated for the public good. She's in charge of a consumer protection agency called DeWilde's Bunch."

"Very good."

"Yes. Only so far, her research into the credulity gas has turned up nothing. Nothing new in the smog. The androids don't give off anything to speak of. The gas the Melt-O-Mobiles give off when they dissipate seems harmless, at least as far as the laboratory animals are concerned." He lowered his head and whispered, "Personally, I think Heavenly has something to do with it."

"Why?"

"I haven't heard from her for a while. Maybe she's working for Will. He would pay her a lot of money to develop something like this. Besides, a credulity gas is her kind of trick. Anything to stick it to her old man. She has the education and the talent. That's one of the things I want you to check."

"She won't talk to you, I suppose."

"Not in words you'd hear at a tea party."

"I can talk to her right now. What's her number?"

Mr. Daise considered that. I'd never before seen a camel with a furrowed brow. He told me her number and I dialed it on the phone on the desk.

The number rang for a while, and then a man answered. I asked for Heavenly Daise. When I told him who was calling he was silent long enough to have a slow careful thought, and then he asked me to wait.

"Hello?" Heavenly Daise said. Her voice sounded just the way I remembered it: warm, polished, and hard as diamond. She was a slim woman with mounds of red ringlets for hair. The last time I'd seen her was in this very room. She'd looked a little tired, having spent most of a long night in a police station fielding questions she didn't want to answer.

"This is Zoot Marlowe."

"So Slamma-Jamma said. What do you want?" She didn't sound glad to hear from me.

Slamma-Jamma was the big golden robot Heavenly lived with. I still didn't know whether the two of them were into unnatural acts or were just friends.

"I wondered how you and Iron Will were getting along."

"What makes you think we're getting along at all?"

"You're one of the best research biologists around. I understand you're not working for your father. Will Industries would be a logical place for you to go."

She laughed and said, "You're cute when you're working on a case, Marlowe."

"You left out that I'm as subtle as a wrecking ball."

"I guess I did at that. I don't know why I'm telling you this, Marlowe. Maybe for old time's sake. The truth is, I'm not half the android designer Iron's son Whipper is. Talk to him. Talk to both of them. Now that I think of it, talk to anybody but me."

"You're doing what at the moment?"

"I don't see that's any of your business. And that goes double for my father. If you happen to see him you can tell him I said so." The phone clicked loudly, and I listened to the static for a moment while I wondered what this conversation had to do with my life.

When I hung up Mr. Daise said, "What did she say?"

"It's none of your business. It's none of my business. And just in case anybody should ask, it's none of their business either."

"Is she working for Will?"

"She says not."

"Do you believe her?"

"Do you know of any reason for her to lie?"

"She doesn't need a reason."

"Look, Mr. Daise. Say she's working for Mr. Will. So what? You can't control her actions. You even need help talking to her on the phone."

Mr. Daise chewed for a while and then said, "All right." He was quiet for a long time. I could actually hear him chewing. The smell in the room did not improve with age. I said, "Is that it? One phone call?"

"No. I want you to follow Mr. Will. See where he goes, what he does, who he talks to."

"Industrial espionage is a little out of my line."

"I'll make it worth your while."

I smiled and said, "Maybe you're right, Mr. Daise. Maybe I'm not half the detective you think I am." I turned and strolled toward the door.

"I know you, Marlowe. You'll end up working on this for free. Just because you don't like Iron Will any more than I do. I'll tell Carla DeWilde to expect you."

I put my hand on the doorknob and turned to look at him, or at what he was at the moment. I said, "You may be right at that." Bill and I left the library. Davenport appeared from somewhere and handed me a piece of paper as he let us out the door.

Bill and I stood on the front step for a moment. I don't know what Bill was doing but I was enjoying the fresh smell of the bright morning. The big brown car was still there, still making my Belvedere look like something you'd get from a cereal box.

Mr. Daise hadn't hired me after all. Officially, I was still without a case, but I didn't feel idle. I felt that I was being sucked down into a pit that would take plenty of work to climb out of. And there was no guarantee I would make it. I opened the paper. On it was Carla DeWilde's address. Not knowing why, I put it into my pocket.

"Home," I said to Bill.

"Right, Boss," he said.

The drive to Malibu was long but pleasant. Not more than three or four bright boys in small foreign cars tried to cut me off. Only one truck hugged my tail, trying to make me drive faster on a road just crowded enough that driving faster was not possible. After breathing the gamy air in Mr. Daise's library, Los Angeles air actually seemed clean.

I pulled into the garage, and when I cut the motor I heard the sounds of insurrection. People were shouting and bouncing off walls. Big animals growled. I hurried across the garden and into the house with Bill behind me. When I got to the living room I stopped, startled. Bill cried, "Cowabunga!"

I'm good, but even I'm not used to walking into the blades of a food processor.

7

Anecdotal Evidence

Bill would have joined the fray if I hadn't grabbed him ever so gently by the neck.

It was a scene out of an old silent comedy—if you didn't mind taking your comedy with a teaspoon of menace. Zamp and the surfers were jumping over furniture trying to stay out of the way of mustard yellow cats the size of tigers, but each one having a pair of long teeth like daggers—useful for opening cans or other victims. Around the necks of the cats were blue plastic collars.

The saber-toothed cats seemed to be herding my relative and friends into the arms of tall, good-looking androids. In the excitement I couldn't tell how many androids or android cats there were, but it was more than I could handle with both hands. Or even with both hands and a gun. Which, at the moment, I did not have. Not even a squirt gun.

"Help!" Zamp cried.

The androids noticed me then and a couple of them closed in. Rougher than he had to, one of them pushed Bill aside. Bill squawked, "Boss!"

but he seemed to be out of harm's way for the moment, so I told him to stay where he was. I backed along the hallway. Without a whip and a chair, what could I do?

The front door was only a few feet away. I wondered if I could get it open before the androids rushed me. Somebody at the back of my brain was trying to tell me something important that just yesterday had not seemed very important at all. I couldn't hear what he was saying. If all these people would stop shouting and running around I could hear and—

Then I remembered. "Bill," I cried, "those are androids. Give 'em the old whoop."

"Right, Boss. Whooping is my business." He whooped as he had the day before while he'd polished surf-bots with the surfers. The noise got everybody's attention right away, but the androids tried to ignore it. Mine kept after me. The noise of frenzied collecting continued in the living room. Then Zamp and the others caught on and they began to whoop too. The androids and android cats didn't look any more bothered, so I said to Bill, "Louder."

"Volume coming up." He punched big holes in the air with his whoops, causing the androids to stop and shake their heads, while the cats howled with a noise like the tearing of tin sheets. They looked a little more interested in getting away from Bill and a little less interested in rounding up folks.

"Louder," I said.

Bill just nodded. He was giving me a headache, but I didn't stop him. The androids and android cats hurried out the back door. The surfers ran after them shaking their mighty fists. I grabbed Bill and ran back to my car. I opened the garage door, and seconds later a big SA truck went by with three androids in the front seat. It rolled south on PCH, making good time. Bill and I rolled after the truck.

Bill was still whooping and he seemed to enjoy it. I tapped him on the shoulder and gave him the cut-throat signal. He gave it back to me. Between whoops I cried, "Stop!" and Bill sort of ran down. At last, he squeaked to a stop.

The android driving the truck was good, probably because his superpower was driving in traffic. His truck was three or four times the size of my Chevy, but he drove it as if it were a Porsche. Using some fancy patterns of acceleration and near-stopping, he wove in and out of traffic holes that looked to be too small for a skateboard. I got farther and farther behind, and eventually I was cut off the trail by a red light and some very emphatic cross-traffic.

Using more care than I had on the way out, I drove back to Whipper's house. There was no mystery for me here. Unless those surfers had suddenly become prime hostage material, it was obvious that Mr. Will was behind the attempted abduction. Just making good his threat. Good old reliable Mr. Will.

Still, as far as the police would be concerned I had no evidence. Anybody could order an android to kidnap somebody. Those saber-toothed cats were a nice feature, but I couldn't make them mean anything. Of course, if I'd caught the truck I might have had something for the police to chew on. But I would have had to pitch it against Mr. Will's money and his influence and his friends downtown. I might as well have thrown flowers at a tank.

When I got back to the house the surfers and Zamp were in the living room discussing their brave stand. Thumper told me I was an aggro dude and everybody else agreed.

Bingo stood near Whipper, looking as angry as a festering sore. Whipper spoke into the phone, his voice quivering with emotion but otherwise under control: "Of course I'm cranked. What did you, like, expect? That was grotty, Dad. I mean, I'm really dogged, dissed, and drilled." He listened. "Ha!" Whipper said. Then, "Don't try to snake me. I'll never come back to Will Industries. You can jam on it." He hung up in Mr. Will's face hard enough to make the bell ring on this end.

Whipper stood there with his hand on the receiver. To nobody in particular he said, "Dad says he didn't do it. He sounds top-to-bottom, and it doesn't seem like his kind of gig, but who else would throw down a raw rap like this?"

"He did it," Bingo said quietly, a volcano clearing its throat to remind you it was still there. "You can bet on it."

Whipper noticed me and said, "Swift thinking, Holmes."

"I didn't catch them."

"What if you had?" Bingo said.

She was right, of course. Could I pull them over and make them wait for the police? Could I chain the androids together and put muzzles on the cats? I had just chased them to have something to do.

Whipper said, "They'll be back. You working on a case, dude?"

I thought about Mr. Daise and the androids and the gas. I said, "Not as such."

Without much trouble Whipper hired me as bodyguard for the whole surfing set, Grampa Zamp included. No money was mentioned, but I was still getting room and board, and now Zamp was too.

When that was settled, I said to Whipper, "I'm going to see Carla DeWilde. Want to come?"

"Huh? The consumer protection dudette? Why?"

"Knighten Daise says she's researching credulity gas. He thinks it has something to do with androids. You're my android expert."

When I mentioned androids he got a little cagey. "I thought you didn't have a case."

"I'm supposed to be protecting you from whoever ordered the attack on the house. Just for simplicity's sake and to keep it in the family, let's say it was your father. When he was here he seemed a little upset that the gas didn't work on you or on the other surfers. And if the gas is connected with androids some way it would be convenient. Wouldn't it?"

"Right on," Bingo said, and nodded.

Whipper tried to smile. "And a connection like that would please Knighten Daise too."

"Probably. But what pleases Mr. Daise is not my largest concern."

Whipper was convinced. While he and I got ready to go, I told Bill to stay behind. "If you see androids again, whoop it up like you did before."

"Right, Boss." Bill began to whoop. I gave him the cut-off sign. He did it back again, but this time he stopped whooping.

As Whipper and I were walking out the door the phone rang. Bingo answered, not her usual warm self, I thought. Evidently it wasn't Mr. Will, because instead of gnawing on the receiver and spitting out the pieces, she handed it to Whipper. He mumbled and nodded into the phone for a while, and then we left. In the car I handed him Carla DeWilde's address. He grunted and told me it was in the valley, not very far out.

We went north through the hills to pick up the Ventura Freeway. The brush and scrub gave the air the sweet dusty fragrance that only California hills have. We went around a hairpin and Whipper said, "On the blower was Mr. Enyart of the aggro new Malibu Tenants Association. Night after next they're meeting to talk about Max Toodemax."

"That ought to impress him."

"We can't just let him dog us."

"He probably doesn't expect you to let him.

But he won't let you dog him either. That gives you sort of a problem in common."

Whipper shrugged and said, "I don't think it'll help."

Whimsical fool that I am, I said, "Max Toodemax and your father are probably personal friends."

Whipper shook his head and stared out the window.

On the other side of the hills the air was much hotter, and you could see it better. It had a hard chemical smell and caught in my throat, making breathing a bit of an effort. Breathing would be an effort even if you didn't have my nose. The nasty smell of the credulity gas teased me, but it never became stronger than the smell of romance the morning after. Melt-O-Mobile dispensers were few and far between. Evidently Mr. Will's products had not yet caught on in the valley.

Whipper got me down onto Ventura Boulevard, where a minimall was on every corner that did not have a gas station. Had I been hungry, I could have eaten Italian, Indian, Thai, or if I searched long enough, even American. Buildings of two or three stories could be had in any color as long as it was pink or white.

The address we were looking for was four stories high and entirely fronted with glass, making it match the medical buildings on either side. That would be Mr. Daise's idea of security. All that glass didn't seem to bother him.

I drove around to the back, where I traded quips with a guard who would not let us into the parking lot until I mentioned that I was a friend of Mr. Daise here to see Carla DeWilde. He called somebody on a telephone and a moment later I was looking for a place to park. The lot was crowded. Melt-O-Mobiles were obviously no more popular among DeWilde's Bunch than they were with the valley's other residents. I found a spot under a eucalyptus tree whose trunk was shedding bark that looked like scraps of paper. Its clean smell was given a hard metallic edge by the smog.

Whipper sweated a few quarts of water crossing the lot, and then we were freezing inside the building. Carla DeWilde's office was on the top floor.

We rode up with a short fat guy carrying Chinese food in a brown paper bag almost as tall as he was. The fourth floor hallway was plain and painted the piercing yellow of a mad dog's eyes. Gray hunks of lab equipment stood against the walls. In one of the rooms, somebody laughed. An intense woman ran from one room to another taking only enough notice of her surroundings not to run into them.

We found Carla DeWilde's office and went into a small room the same color as the hallway, though somebody had tried to hide the walls with prints of mountains rising above serene forests. A thin woman behind a metal desk asked us to wait for a moment. She had a voice no larger than she was. We sat in folding chairs, trying to warm the metal with our bottoms. The floor was a swirl of unhappy green that had seen a lot of use.

"Mr. Marlowe?"

Whipper and I looked up. Standing at the door to the inner office was a robot the same bronze color as the Daises' robotler. It was substantial—nobody's idea of a ballet dancer—but it had the unmistakable curves of a woman. Hair nearly the same color as her brightwork was piled on top of her head. A lab coat was painted on over a red dress, which was painted on too. Holding her hair in place was an SSR headband. Of course.

In a voice like a tiny glass bell, Carla DeWilde invited us into her office, which was a little bigger than the waiting room but crowded with paper, thick books, and more lab equipment. Stacks of files covered her desk. She introduced herself and shook hands—surprisingly warm but not very soft—then sat with her back to a picture window that would have given her a good view of the hills if the smog had not trailed across them like a dirty veil.

"Whipper Will?" she said with her eyebrows up.

Whipper said, "Yes," as if admitting he drew mustaches on monuments but was proud of it.

"Aren't you in the camp of your enemy?"

"Dad and I are not so cool at the moment. I'm just here with Zoot—Mr. Marlowe."

She looked at me and smiled with all her

teeth. They were perfect. She said, "Mr. Daise said I could expect you."

"He doesn't lack anything but insecurity, does he?"

"No." She glanced at Whipper again. He really bothered her.

I said, "Look, Ms. DeWilde, Whipper knows a lot more about androids than I do. He's here because he might ask a question that I wouldn't even think of. But let's say he's a spy for his father. Let's say when he leaves here, he'll run tell Mr. Will that you know something nobody knows you know. Do you know anything worth the price of a phone call?"

She made a quick drum roll on the desk with her fingers. I don't know why SSR designed robots to act nervous but they did a good job of it. Eventually she stopped drumming and said, "Mr. Daise told me to talk to you. What do you want to know?"

"A lot of people seem to think there's some connection between the credulity gas and the androids and the Melt-O-Mobiles. My guess is that even Mr. Will thinks so, though he doesn't talk about it much."

DeWilde sighed very realistically. She didn't say anything but rummaged under her desk and came up a moment later with a thin book that had a black pebbled cover. She opened it and absentmindedly turned the loose-leaf pages, browsing as if she were alone and killing an afternoon. People passed in the hallway. Somewhere a filing cabinet clicked shut. DeWilde said, "We have a lot of evidence that the credulity gas exists, but it's not what we'd call scientific evidence."

"What would we call it?" Whipper said.

"It's anecdotal. Just reports by untrained observers under conditions that were far from controlled."

"Enough of even that kind of evidence should mean something," I said.

DeWilde shook her head. "Enough was never enough for flying saucers."

She was right, of course. If she hadn't been, I would have become an exhibit at Pasadena Tech a long time ago. I said, "I've seen it work."

"More anecdotal evidence." The thought of hearing my story did not excite her.

Whipper said, "*You* must be doing controlled experiments."

She would have blushed had she been able. She stood up, said, "Come on. I'll show you something," and walked out of the room.

We followed her down the hallway to an open doorway at the end of it. Inside was a big room with lab benches down one long side. One short wall was glass. Beyond the glass were two smaller rooms. Inside one, seated in a chair, was an android. It looked faded and a little ratty—like a doll that had been out in the weather too long. Inside the other was a Melt-O-Mobile. Watching the two small rooms were people in lab coats sitting behind control panels.

DeWilde said, "How old would you say that android is?"

"At least six months," Whipper said.

"We've had it nearly that long. The Melt-O-Mobile is new. Go ahead, Charlie."

Charlie did something to his control panel and the Melt-O-Mobile began to fizz. While it disappeared, DeWilde said, "We've done every test we can think of on both of them. As the android goes stale it gives off a gas with a complicated formula but which seems to have no effect on any animal we've tried, up to and including humans." She peered hard at me. I tried to look as human as possible.

DeWilde smiled. "We call the gas *android cooties.*" The smile was gone as if it had never been, and she went on. "The gas the Melt-O-Mobiles effervesce into is different, but it is also benign. After testing them separately we mixed the two gases in various proportions. Still nothing significant. As far as we can determine, if there is a credulity gas neither androids nor Melt-O-Mobiles have anything to do with it."

I looked at Whipper. He was looking at the floor. Maybe he was thinking. Maybe he was just looking for paper clips. He didn't seem happy about it.

I thanked Carla DeWilde. She asked us to remember her if we dug up anything she could use—something more than anecdotal, I suppose—and we left.

The drive back to Malibu was quiet. We were

almost at the Topanga Canyon offramp when Whipper said, "I told you Dad was OK."

I agreed with him to the extent of saying, "You did."

When we got back to Malibu Zamp and Bill ran out to the garage to meet us. Bill was his usual self but Zamp was no gayer than a funeral barge. He said, "The androids came back. They got everybody."

8

Everything but the Girl

Of course, they hadn't gotten everybody. Bill and Grampa Zamp were still here. Zamp had been out surfing with a bot that Mustard had loaned him. By the time Bill ran out to get him the house was already empty.

Whipper and Zamp and I righted the furniture that had fallen over, then we stood in the middle of the living room making the nervous purposeless gestures that people make when they don't know what to do. Bill was sitting on the couch. Not much bothered him, but I thought this might. He'd failed me.

Whipper asked the question before I had a chance to. He said, "Didn't we tell you to whoop?"

"Sure. I remember. Bubble memory." His bubble memory pleased him.

Whipper stroked his forehead.

I said, "Did you whoop, Bill?"

"Sure. I whooped loud."

"And the androids took everybody away anyhow."

"Right, Boss."

I looked at Whipper. He looked at me. Together, we said, "Earplugs!"

Whipper threw himself into a chair and held his head in his hands. He mumbled.

"What?" Zamp said.

He looked at a place between me and Zamp, the strain making his face look like a crushed paper cup. He nearly shouted: "This isn't like Dad. It's not his style."

"Did you have another suspect in mind?"

"You're the detective, dammit!"

I didn't say anything. Nothing clever enough came to mind. I saw Zamp glance at me, but instead of saying anything he sat at one end of the couch.

Whipper leapt to his feet and ran to the kitchen, where he called the police. Back in the living room he sat down, stood up, sat down again. He looked around the room as if he knew clues were there somewhere, hidden like Easter eggs. "They made a mistake," he said.

I grunted. He didn't want to hear me talk anyway.

"They took Bingo."

He almost couldn't say her name. He stopped looking for clues and studied the dust in one corner of the room. Probably he wasn't looking at the dust at all.

"What—?" Zamp began. I waved him into silence and said, "We're not entirely without options here."

Whipper said nothing. He barely breathed.

" 'Oh no?' you say. 'No,' says I."

This did nothing to perk him up.

I said, "Your father took the surfers as hostages because he wants you to improve the androids for him. You could go back to work for him. It could buy us some time."

"Time?" Whipper said, not quite daring to be interested.

"If you go back he'll probably take reasonable care of Bingo and the others, holding their welfare over you until he gets what he wants. If you don't go back he's liable to do something desperate, if only to prove he means business."

Not really angry at *me*, Whipper shouted, "This isn't like him. He's a businessman, not a gangster."

I wanted to suggest that people change but decided not to bother. Quietly I said, "Did you have any other suspects?"

He shook his head.

I said, "Call him. Tell him you're coming back to work. It'll buy us time."

We sat in the living room for a long while. Even with the four of us there it seemed to be a lot emptier than it was. The walls radiated loneliness. Outside, people talked and joked up and back. Wind blew, and the surf, as surf will, continued to crawl in from Japan. The sea breeze was touched with credulity gas but no harder than with a mother's kiss.

Whipper went into the kitchen and punched more numbers. He said, "This is Whipper Will. I want to talk to my father." A moment later, he said, "I don't care what kind of meeting he's in. After what happened, he owes me a little of his time." Another moment rumbled by like a heavy truck. Whipper made a noise that might have been a bad word and the phone was slammed back into its cradle. He stood in the doorway between the living room and the kitchen, nothing in his eyes but hatred and pain, if eyes ever contain anything at all.

Whipper said, "All of a sudden he's playing hard to get. He's in meetings, getting ready for the trade show tonight."

"He'll be there?"

"That's what she said."

"We'll go."

Zamp said, "We only have two free tickets.'

"Whipper and I have to go."

Zamp's nose twitched. He said, "They're *my* tickets."

I knew that eventually we would be forced to buy another ticket, but I didn't have time to mention it because somebody knocked at the front door. It was a polite knock, but it would want answering. Unless it was somebody selling religion or encyclopedias, it could only be the police.

They came in, smooth and professional as a well-oiled engine. There were three of them, two in uniform and one in a brown suit. The one in the suit even wore a hat, which was unusual enough for California, but over his arm he carried a trench coat that in the Malibu heat was as useful as a butter churn. He was tall enough for basketball and wide enough for boxing. A chin like a brick and twinkling eyes made him look like a TV detective. Some people might have trouble taking him seriously.

"Sergeant Preston," he said, and shook hands all around. While Bill pumped him, I said wonderingly, "Of the Yukon?"

He looked at me as if he'd expected better and said, "No. Of the valley."

Whipper was in no mood, but I laughed. "Very quick," I said.

"Not really," Sergeant Preston said. "I've been asked that question before. Mind if we look around?" He pried himself loose from Bill and put his hand into a pocket.

"Clues," Whipper said, and nodded.

The uniformed boys went to work while Sergeant Preston sat down and took out a notebook. He licked the tip of a pencil and asked us to tell our story. Zamp did most of the talking. Then Sergeant Preston said, "What about the bot?"

"Tell him what happened, Bill," I said.

"What happened," Bill told him.

Sergeant Preston's eyebrows went up and Whipper shook his head. He looked even more tired than I felt. I said, "Tell him about when the androids took away the surfers."

"Sure, Boss. I know that one," Bill said proudly, and he began. To the astonishment of everybody in the room, Bill played it back exactly as it happened. We heard the shouts of the surfers, Bill's whoops, furniture falling over, heavy running. Bill made a sound like a door slam that was so realistic it was all I could do not to check if somebody had just come in. He said, "The end," and stopped.

Sergeant Preston laughed and closed his notebook. "If we don't find anything, we might have him do that into a tape recorder."

I shook my head and said, "I knew radio would make a comeback."

Sergeant Preston stood up and said, "Patter. I've heard about you."

"Me?" I said, genuinely surprised and immediately suspicious.

"A short guy with a beak who solves crimes. Not the beak, the guy. I hear that trouble is your business."

"I'd like to stop, but you know how trouble is."

He frowned at the carpet and looked at me. "Chandler fan?"

"I guess I don't hide it very well."

"Me too." He shook hands with me again, but this time he meant it.

The uniformed policemen came back to him and said they'd gotten all they could out of the room, which wasn't much.

At the front door Sergeant Preston turned to me and said, "You plan on looking into this?"

"I don't want to step on any toes." Which was not an answer and he knew it.

"No, no. Go right ahead. But if anything turns up remember you have friends downtown."

I told him I would. He and the uniformed

types got into a police car and went away. They didn't use the siren, but people stayed out of their way anyhow.

The afternoon was long. Whipper spent most of it out in back, facing a scene that people from the middle of the country paid big bucks to see—water, sand, healthy bodies not too weighted down with clothes. To him it was just another day at the beach.

I wanted to go out and do some detecting, but I didn't know where to start. My investigations into credulity gas seemed to have hit a brick wall. I could call Mr. Daise and tell him that, but he might get the impression I was working for him. He would feel he had the right to chew me out. I wasn't in the mood to be chewed on.

I could have searched for Bingo and the other surfers. If Mr. Will was not behind the abduction, I had no idea who might be. Evidently searching the house had not told the professionals much either. I could have spent the afternoon at Willville, wherever it was, but Mr. Will's security people would certainly not be amused at my poking sticks under private rocks. That might hurt the surfers more than help them. I'd end up at Willville eventually, of course, but I wanted to talk to Mr. Will first. Kind of by mistake-like, he might drop a clue that might tell me which rock to poke under.

The Sun crawled down the sky, sneaking up on the horizon, and the breeze turned cool. Whipper went out for chicken and brought it back in a cardboard box as substantial as a Melt-O-Mobile. We ate the chicken, but we would have gotten as much pleasure eating the box. Nobody spoke. We just ate because we had to eat.

When we were done Whipper got into the loudest Hawaiian shirt he owned and we were ready to go. He rode shotgun and Zamp sat in back with Bill, who gave directions to the Convention Center.

It was the kind of silky Southern California night the Chamber of Commerce would like to bottle and send to Chicago in the winter. It smelled of the sea and wild, impetuous high jinks. The sky was the usual gray blanket, but the ocean sparkled as if stars were floating just under the surface.

I turned toward downtown on the Santa Monica Freeway. Traffic was light, the way Caltrans would have you believe it would be if they were allowed to build just one more freeway. Just one more. And then another one.

We drifted east and slowed at a traffic knot that we rode in bumper to bumper until I got off and maneuvered along one-way streets that were crowded with big cars riding much too low to the ground. The big dark shapes of buildings hunched over us showing lights where offices were being cleaned. The smell of credulity gas tickled my nostrils like the blade of a knife. It seemed to be everywhere now, but here it was not strong enough to work. At least none of the open stores were being mobbed.

The traffic was heavy and became heavier as we approached a building with searchlights revolving in front. I crept around the block, just one more turtle in the parade, and went under a marquee that announced WILL INDUSTRIES PRESENTS ITS TRADE SHOW: THE FUTURE IS HERE. Whipper tried not to sneer but failed. I entered a driveway where a guy took three bucks, handed me a card that said the company wasn't responsible for anything, and told me to park anywhere. He looked impatiently behind me for the next customer.

I parked anywhere, as directed, and got out of the car. Whipper, Zamp, Bill, and I followed the crowd to a bank of escalators. Whipper, Zamp and I almost lost him while Bill tried to figure out where the steps came from. I wouldn't let him march down the up escalator, though he tried.

Above was a lobby with a lot of open doors and even more ticket windows. Zamp and I watched people pass while Whipper stood in line to buy a ticket. Zamp was fascinated. Bouncy music came through the doorways. He craned his head to look inside but couldn't see much.

"Nothing like this on T'toom," he said, and sighed.

"Too much of it on Earth," I said.

"You know, Zoot, you'd be a happier person if you weren't so cynical."

"I've tried, but I can't seem to get the knack."

He looked sideways at me and said, "The patter, yes." He sighed again, more hugely this time. He said, "Thanks for bringing me to Earth."

"You may be sorry yet."

He smiled and said, "I'll let you know."

Whipper came over to us with a red cardboard oblong in his hand. We queued up at a door, but when it got to be our turn the woman wouldn't let Bill in. He didn't have a ticket.

"He's just a robot," I said.

She was a round woman with black hair that looked as if it had been glued in place. Her gray uniform did not fit her very well. I got the feeling that nothing would. She said, "A robot. A Surfing Samurai Robot. Yeah. He'll need a ticket."

For a moment I considered leaving Bill in the lobby, then went to get him a ticket. We went in at the same door, but the round woman didn't seem to remember us. She took Bill's ticket along with ours without comment.

Beyond the doors was a room not quite as large as Dodger Stadium—a dance floor for giants. The edges and corners were lost in blackness, but islands of light dotted the floor, each one featuring a different Will Industries product being fondled by a woman wearing an outfit that had to be expensive because there was so little of it. Air from outside had been piped in, chilled, and seasoned with a little ancient cigarette smoke and the shampoo they'd used on the rugs that afternoon; only a Toomler would have noticed it. I was surprised not to smell credulity gas.

Androids walked through the crowd giving out literature and free samples, answering questions, laughing at jokes. I guess their superpower was getting along with strangers. The androids were all dressed up, but the tuxedoes were designed to leave their necks bare so we could see the blue plastic collars.

At one end of the room was a stage that would look small only here. The original cast of Napoleon's invasion of Russia would have gotten lost on it. At each end of it was a loud speaker no larger than a church door. In the middle of the stage a young man in jeans and a T-shirt sat behind a control board, moving with the bouncy music. Near him, a record was spinning. I guessed that's where the music was coming from.

In a curve that swept across the stage in front of the young man were five Melt-O-Mobiles. Each vehicle was accompanied by a matching Melt-O-Mobile dispenser on a turntable that spun slower than the second hand of a clock. If you wanted one, you could get a good look at the merchandise.

Near the front of the stage was a sixth turntable with another car on it. That would be the expensive model. Riding the hood was Darken Stormy, her smile bright enough to take flash pictures by. She'd gotten her outfit at the same store as the other girls, but it was tighter where it would do the most good, and short enough for a telegram. Her dark hair fell like night except where the red highlights showed through from another universe. She spoke into a microphone and writhed across the car as it turned, so she always faced the audience. The green fish scales of her dress sparkled under the spotlight as she moved. Swell hood ornament. If I'd been a human male she'd be the one who would make me howl and do nip-ups, and then I'd buy a car. A lot of guys in the crowd looked as if that's what they had in mind.

Darken said, "The new Melt-O-Mobile runs on regular unleaded gas, and best of all, you never have to park it." She gave us a smile they could use to kick-start a nuclear reactor. "Push one button and the Melt-O-Mobile just disappears." More smile. "It evaporates into a harmless, inert gas. Actual tests show that it is environmentally sound and nonpolluting. To get another car, merely use one of the Melt-O-Mobile dispensers located conveniently all over the city."

I wondered if they'd gotten the part about *actual tests* from Carla DeWilde. Or whether the advertising department just liked the sound of it.

Whipper nudged me and said, "Let's find Dad." I nodded and we moved among the reefs of people. Most of them seemed pretty happy, maybe even ready to buy something. Music and pretty girls and somebody laughing at your jokes would do that to you, I guess. Like Zamp had said, we didn't have anything like this on T'toom.

At one corner of the room was a small reception area, hardly worth mentioning, only the size of a basketball court. A lot of guys in suits stood around smiling while they waited for their pensions. A few of them were at desks across from civilians, working out on what was probably a bill of sale. Sitting on a platform—no more than a bump under the rug, really—sat a man in a high-backed swivel chair. It would be a very comfortable chair. The man was Iron Will. He waved at people as they went by. Some of them shook his hand and told him what a swell party this was. He agreed with whatever they said. That's the kind of guy Iron Will was.

While we watched him from a dim spot out on the main floor, Whipper licked his lips and said, "I don't know what's going to happen. I'm scared."

"Probably wise," I said. "Want to go home?"

Instead of answering me, he said, "Listen Zoot, you're an aggro dude. A good guy. A person I can trust. Find Bingo and the others. I don't want to work for him any longer than I have to."

"If the right intentions were all it took, we wouldn't even be here. Got any good ideas?"

"Something will come," he said hurriedly. Maybe he was afraid of losing his nerve. "And go to that neighborhood meeting."

"Is that part of the case?"

A little nastily, Whipper said, "If you want to continue having a place to sleep, it is."

Sure. And I could stop a charging elephant with my piercing gaze.

When we approached, Mr. Will actually had the presence of mind to look surprised. He got up and took Whipper's hand in both of his. "Whipper, my boy. How nice to see you." He nodded at me and Zamp. "And your friends too." He frowned. "Though, perhaps the robot was uncalled for."

Whipper said. "Like, I'm here, Dad. I'm ready to wire your stuff."

"Must you talk like that?"

Whipper smiled. It was nothing compared to Darken Stormy's smile, but it wasn't bad under the circumstances.

"Very well," Mr. Will said. He made a casual motion with one hand and two androids walked up. They were big and had chins like anvils but no foreheads at all. Their dark hair was slicked straight back with something that smelled as heavy and sweet as the underside of a bear rug. Maybe their superpower was the strange ability to beat somebody to a pulp if he tried to escape. They lined up on either side of Whipper, and Mr. Will said, "I'd like to know what changed your mind about coming back to work."

I thought Whipper would only smile again, but he leaned toward his dad and said, "If you hurt them even a little bit, both you and your androids will rot."

Mr. Will's face showed no more response than a peeled egg. He only gestured and the two Neanderthal androids led Whipper away. Mr. Will

didn't even watch. He contemplated me and
Zamp and Bill. He put on his Sunday smile for
us and said, "What do you think of the show?"

I looked around, not really seeing anything. I
said, "I guess it's all for sale."

"Everything but the girl," Mr. Will said, and
laughed louder than the gag deserved. He kept
laughing. Bill chuckled just to keep him company. Zamp and I shrugged.

Still chuckling to himself, Mr. Will said, "I
think you could cause me a great deal of trouble, Mr. Marlowe."

I stiffened, expecting a couple of his android
goons to grab me. I might as well have whistled
like a cuckoo bird. Mr. Will just waved his hand
over his head as if making a playing card appear.

Onstage, Darken Stormy rolled off the Melt-
O-Mobile and said, "You'll never have to park
again!" She reached into the car and then
backed away from it, making a here's-the-big-
deal motion with her hands. The car began to
evaporate and I smelled the credulity gas.

Mr. Will cried out, "This is Zoot Marlowe.
He's a bad man. He deserves to die."

All around, people who had been ignoring me
looked in my direction with blood in their eyes.
They began to close in.

9

You Can Fool All of the People Some of the Time

These people were not trained killers. Most of them looked soft as goose-down pillows. A few of them were no more than kids. But there were a lot of them. They could bury me alive if they didn't tear me apart first.

I told Bill and Zamp to back away from me. Bill followed orders instantly, but Zamp didn't move till I hollered at him, a little hysterically.

It was the credulity gas, of course. The air was suddenly lousy with it. Despite what Carla DeWilde said, despite Will Industries' *actual tests,* the gas obviously was as well connected with the Melt-O-Mobile as two freight cars were connected to the Twentieth Century Limited. In its present condition, that crowd would believe I was Jack the Ripper or Jessie James or a plate of spaghetti, large, with plenty of garlic. I called out, "Wait. I'm just some guy. Even looking at me is boring."

Members of the crowd wavered. Their eyes

wandered. The wall of flesh broke up like a head of dandelion fuzz in the wind.

Behind me, Mr. Will cried, "He killed your children! He doesn't deserve to live!"

Once more I became the object of their affection. They began to close in again, but it was early. A hole was still open off to one side. I darted through it, smooth as a greased mouse, and ran for the stage. The crowd trailed a tall thin guy, yelling and waving their arms like Hollywood natives in an old Tarzan picture. The thin guy grabbed for me, but I made it to the main stage. Darken tried to stop me but I pushed her into the thin guy—a moment he would probably remember fondly—and ran to the control board.

The kid spinning the records looked frightened. That was good. That was just fine. Evidently he hadn't heard what Mr. Will had said about me. "Scram," I yelled, and he backed away, uncertain what I would do with his equipment.

I was uncertain myself, never having seen a setup like this. It was more complicated than the controls of my sneeve and it had no computer. I yelled, "There he goes, the baby-killer!" I pointed at the other end of the auditorium.

Everybody ran in the direction I'd pointed. Everybody. All the people who'd been chasing me, the sound technician, and even Darken Stormy. She was a little wobbly on her high heels, but she managed to keep up. Very handy stuff, this credulity gas.

Before Mr. Will could tell my pursuers any different I turned all the dials on the board toward the high numbers. The bouncy tune beat on my eardrums with hammers, even behind the speakers where I was. The bass rattled and buzzed. I saw Mr. Will down on the floor yelling into ears, but it was doing him no good. Zamp and Bill hurried up to me, and I led them to the back of the stage. We found a door marked EXIT, and did what it said.

We hustled along a wide yellow corridor that bent around the main auditorium. The bright fluorescent light bled the color out of everything and made my head hurt. It was a hard shadowless place, without comfort, without hope. One light in three flickered and hummed like an angry insect. There were no doors, no cross corridors, no places to hide, no way out. Nothing but that wide yellow corridor.

I heard shouts behind us and running footsteps. It could have been two people or a dozen. They were hidden by the curve of the corridor.

"What's going on?" Zamp said between gasps.

"First we'll run, then we'll talk." I didn't sound so athletic myself. Bill stepped along without fatigue.

We passed a large industrial kitchen, shining with polished aluminum countertops. We could hide in there, but if something went wrong we'd be boxed in. I kept running. And found what I'd been waiting for. It was another door marked EXIT.

I pulled open the door and got Zamp and Bill

inside. We were in a stairwell. The air in it was deader than ancient Egypt. Careful as a guy trying a jigsaw puzzle piece, I set my ticket stub on one of the upward steps and hoped it would look more convincing to our pursuers than it did to me. We ran down. There was nothing upstairs for us. Downstairs, we'd at least be at street level.

We went down to ONE and out into another corridor. This one was painted a green never seen in nature. I was a little turned around.

"Which way to the front of the building, Bill?"

"Where we came in?"

"Right."

He pointed left and we kept moving.

I'd taken a few steps along the curving corridor when I saw a cross corridor not far ahead. I should have suspected something, if only so we could have a good laugh over it later, but I was too eager to get out of there. Instead of creeping up on the cross corridor like Daniel Boone, or even avoiding the possibility of ambush entirely and going the other way, I just kept running.

At the cross corridor something growled and I looked at it. It was a saber-toothed tiger wearing a blue plastic collar. The three of us froze in midstride, and we looked at the tiger with wide stupid eyes, like rabbits caught in headlights.

In a situation like that you don't do much thinking. You just do what comes natural. The tiger prowled toward us, low and ready to spring, so we backed up. Anything could have been behind us. Gino and Darlene. Count Dracula. A bottomless pit. Nothing at all. We did not look. We were a little preoccupied.

Somebody grabbed me from behind and I heard, "Yikes!" from Zamp. My somebody dragged me down the cross corridor like a sack of potatoes. I looked up over my shoulder and saw the work was being done by an android. Another android was wrestling my Grampa Zamp in the same direction. Bill was watching from the intersection. "Whoop, Bill! Whoop!" I cried, my voice as rough as a rat-tail file.

Bill said, "Right, Boss," and began making a noise that bounced around those hard bright corridors like popcorn in a metal pot. I whooped too. So did Zamp. We all whooped together.

I was hoping the noise would disturb the androids enough that they'd loosen their grips. If I was very lucky they might let go altogether so they could put their hands over their ears. I should have known from the way things had been going that my luck was no better than last month's potato salad. The whooping had no effect on them. They were probably wearing earplugs.

I struggled against the massive strength of the android, then grabbed what I could and squeezed. Nothing. I pulled hard. Something snapped and the android stopped. I looked at my hand and saw that gripped in it was the blue collar. I didn't take time to enjoy this moment, but turned around and pushed the motionless android over with one finger. It fell, making the kind of untidy laundry-bag noise a man makes when he falls.

I cried, "Come on, Bill," and pounded down the corridor after the other android and the tiger that loped at his side. And Zamp. I called, "Tear off his collar!"

But there were too many echoes, and Zamp's arms were pinned, and the damned android moved too fast. I lost them around the curve of the corridor but kept running. After I had run enough I came to a loading dock. The androids hadn't had time to pull the door back down. A truck was pulling away. On the back it said ID ADVERTISING, #82. I could have leapt for the back bumper but breaking my neck would not have done Zamp any good.

Bill came up beside me and I said, "Get the license number."

Bill did his best. He peered after the truck and made his eyes light up, but I knew it was hopeless.

"Too dark, Boss," he said. "Too far away." He managed to sound sorry. Nice of SSR to build a robot that would do that. I needed a little sympathy right then.

10
Truckers Do It All Night

I don't know what I should have done then, but I should have done it fast. I felt as lively as a broken nose. I just sat on the edge of the cement dock watching the taillights get smaller and then turn a corner. I could have run for my car. Ten minutes to find it. Another five to get out of the parking structure. The truck would only be ten or fifteen miles ahead of me in an unknown direction.

I looked at Bill, who was standing and waiting. Good old Bill. Good old reliable robot. I said, "Bill, does your bubble memory have an address for ID Advertising?"

"Sure thing, Boss."

"Don't lose it."

I leapt off the dock and walked around the outside of the building, jumping at every noise. The sidewalk was crowded, but nobody bothered me. I guess whoever wanted anything had everything he wanted. A little something to keep Whipper in line. A little something to keep me in line. I walked down the driveway into the parking structure and found my car. A few minutes later I was following Bill's instructions.

ID Advertising was in Pasadena, beyond the end of the Pasadena Freeway. I must have driven there because we got there, but I didn't notice anything in-between. The car had driven, not me. I was busy hating Mr. Will and telling myself that Zamp would see his abduction as a big adventure. His hot time on old Earth. Mostly I saw his frightened face as the android dragged him up the corridor. Having no tear ducts, I couldn't cry, but I almost managed it anyway.

I thought I knew why Mr. Will had abducted the surfers. I even thought I knew why he'd taken the extra trouble to abduct Zamp. It occurred to me that instead of following the truck I should have hunted for Mr. Will and made his life unpleasant until he told me where everybody was. Then it occurred to me that he had large, powerful employees whose superpower was to make life unpleasant for guys who things occurred to.

ID Advertising was one more one-story building with a plate-glass window in front. The street was not busy, but it wouldn't be at this hour. I turned off the engine and listened to the silence in the car. It was a silence of sorrow and frustration, of which I was the West Coast supplier.

Bill and I got out of the car and walked around to the side of the ID Advertising building, where trucks were parked in neat rows behind a chain-link fence. By walking the entire fence I could see the number on every truck. I didn't see number eighty-two. It wasn't here. It was somewhere else.

I stood outside the fence with my hands in my pockets, feeling silly about coming to Earth, about being a detective, about standing there with my hands in the alien pockets of another man's suit—Philip Marlowe's suit.

I walked back to the car feeling like the inside of a sewer and sat behind the wheel. I must have sat there for a long time because Bill said, "Where to, Boss?"

"We'll wait," I said.

"What are we waiting for?"

It was a logical question, a pretty good question even from somebody who had a much more expensive brain than Bill's. I said, "For truck number eighty-two."

"Waiting is my meat, Boss."

So we waited. It got later. I shut my eyes. I listened to the silence and to the rattling of ideas inside my own head.

What seemed to be a moment later, a growl awakened me. I jumped and hit my head on the ceiling of the car, thinking, in the dream I'd been having, that the tigers were after me again. Bill looked at me sideways and I told him I was all right.

"Sure, Boss," he said, but he kept looking at me.

The growl had been the engine of a truck, of course. I rubbed my eyes as I watched it make a right turn into the driveway of the ID Advertising parking lot. Laboring as if it were pulling the Titanic from the bottom of the ocean, a machine dragged the gate open and then grated as the gate began to shut behind the truck. As the truck turned, a streetlight shone on the back of it. It was number eighty-two. Bill told me it was number eighty-two. That confirmed it.

Bill and I got out of the Belvedere and we ran through the shrinking space between the gate and the fence. Making a sound like a plumber's toolbox falling downstairs, the gate slammed closed behind us. The air was cold, without even a memory of the sun that had warmed it all day. Buried among the jasmine and orange blossoms, other things tickled the inside of my nose: the familiar insult of smog and a vague spicing of credulity gas, fresh as a locker room after the big game.

Bill skipped beside me as I strolled to where the big truck stood, its engine complaining as it died. Like all the other trucks this one was clean, a big cube of vanilla ice cream in the night. I'd missed a few things on it back at the Convention Center. As if it were important, stickers on the rear bumper told me LILLIPUT MINIATURE GOLF and STOP TRUCK STOP and TRUCKERS DO IT ALL NIGHT. That was *all* they told me. Maybe it was some kind of code.

Not knowing what to expect, I rapped on the side of the truck. When nothing happened I rapped again and put the side of my head against the truck. The metal was colder than a penguin's toes. More nothing happened. Then the cab door slammed, making my head ring.

I stood away from the truck, and the driver walked toward me looking very much like a truck himself. He was a man-mountain who stood beside his truck with a pipe that in his hands looked no larger than a toothpick. It was difficult to tell in that light, but I think he had a blue plastic collar around his neck. A superpower is a superpower even if it only allows you to drive a truck better than anybody else.

In that polite way people have when they've caught you and they're being cute about it, he said, "May I help you?"

Knowing it was not smart but being in no mood to be smart, I said, "What's in the truck, bub?" My voice didn't even shake. I just wanted Grampa Zamp back and would likely get my brain parted by this aggro dude for my trouble.

"Nothing but the rent," the driver said, and hefted his pipe.

Bill laughed, but stopped when he saw the dead look on my face.

I rubbed my forenose tiredly and said, "You think it's none of my business, but I lost somebody tonight and I think he might somehow—just by accident, you understand—have gotten into the back of your truck."

"How might he have accidentally done that?" The driver looked puzzled. He might even have been sincere.

"He might have been put there by a couple of

androids, one of whom has very long teeth. But I'm only guessing, of course."

The driver nodded and came toward me with the pipe. Bill and I backed out of his way. He climbed onto the rear bumper of the truck and, with a practiced shove of the heel of his hand, sprung the lock. The door drifted open on hinges that squeaked demurely like a hungry kitten demanding dinner.

Maybe it was because the guy had opened the truck instead of braining me, maybe it was some Toomler extrasense, maybe it was just my imagination, but I *knew* that nothing interesting was inside that truck. I pulled open the door and looked into a space that was about the size of Whipper's bedroom but was considerably emptier. Bill hopped onto the bumper and looked inside too. "Hello?" he called, and made an echo that pleased him. No point my climbing inside. No point giving the driver a chance to lock me in. He might take me to where Zamp and the others were. Or he might just dump me off a freeway overcrossing.

I pulled Bill off the bumper and said, "So, where have you been this evening?"

The driver got cagey. With one finger he wiped imaginary dirt from his truck and said, "Just cruising, mister. That's all. Just cruising."

"In a company truck? In the middle of the night? Not unless your superpower is getting away with stupidity."

He didn't get angry. I'm not sure it was *pos-*

sible for him to get angry. But he took me by
an arm and Bill by an arm and walked us over
to the gate. I didn't have to go. I could have
stood there with one empty shoulder. Using the
toe of one boot he touched a button that opened
the gate and pushed us through—not roughly,
but with the inevitability of a bulldozer.

I turned to watch the gate close. When it was
done and the echo of its slamming died away, I
said, "So there's nobody in your truck, and you
were just out cruising. What do they do in the
office, make paper flowers?"

He looked at the ID Advertising building as if
he'd never seen it before. He said, "I just drive
a truck, you know?"

"Yeah," I said. "I know."

I walked back to the Chevy feeling as black
as the night. Grampa Zamp had trusted me.
Whipper Will had hired me to protect him and
the other surfers. Mr. Daise had not quite hired
me but had presented me with an interesting
problem. Three up. Three down. Only Mr. Will
had come out ahead. Maybe I should send my
bill to him.

I sighed as I settled behind the steering wheel
of the Belvedere feeling like a weathered old
kite hanging from a telephone wire, still a little
gaudy but not much use to anybody. Bill was
as eager to continue as he'd been that morning.
"Where to?" he said.

Bill was my friend, but at the moment his
machinelike persistence angered more than
comforted me. "Dreamland," I said sarcasti-

cally, and knew he would miss the subtle wit. I closed my eyes and tried to get comfortable. On the backs of my closed lids Zamp looked at me more in sadness than in anger.

"I have six Dreamlands in Los Angeles County. Which one did you want?"

If I didn't answer him he'd ask me again in a minute or two. I said, "Forget it, Bill. The one I want isn't in your bubble memory."

"Right, Boss. Forget it."

I must have fallen asleep because when I opened my eyes again, the night had done that funny half-twist it always manages just before sunrise. It was early again. My watch said it was six o'clock.

I couldn't fall back asleep, so I watched Pasadena awaken. There are more exciting things to watch. At nine o'clock a tall woman in a dark blue dress unlocked the glass door of ID Advertising and went inside. Lights came on.

I gave her ten minutes to get the coffee going and to check herself in the mirror. Ten minutes that I measured in geologic ages. I left the car, and Bill fixed the parking meter so I wouldn't have to put change into it. As I was about to push open the glass door I caught a look at my reflection. I was a little gray, and things that had not sagged yesterday sagged now.

I entered a small living room whose walls were painted a bright, almost silver white. The couches against the walls were black furry caterpillars. Over them hung very artistic framed photographs of androids and Melt-O-Mobiles, and sometimes androids and Melt-O-Mobiles together. Lots of shine, lots of sculpted shadows, lots of pretty women lounging against the product and looking very pleased with themselves for knowing how.

The woman in blue must have paid a lot of money to have her blond hair frizzed and piled up on her head in that terrible way. While sitting behind a desk that supported a computer and a telephone she drank coffee from a cup that said WHAT PART OF "NO" DON'T YOU UNDERSTAND? She frowned for a moment, remembered her training, and smiled at me as if she'd had a good night's sleep.

I summoned whatever charm I had left and said, "Good morning. I'm looking for a little information."

She said, "What kind of information?"

Her question was reasonable, but for a moment it stumped me. I waved one hand as if dusting a statue and said, "What do you do here?"

She didn't like that. If I didn't know what went on in this place I couldn't possibly have business. I could see her recede into the distance before she said, "ID Advertising is the advertising arm of Will Industries."

"ID?" I said, sounding confused even to myself.

"Iron Duke, Mr. Will's first and middle names. You've heard of Mr. Will?"

"We've met," I said, confusing *her*. "I'm looking for a friend of mine. He said he would get a ride with truck number eighty-two, but he didn't tell me where it was going." My smile was a thing of thumbtacks and rubber bands and paper clips.

"Our drivers are forbidden to pick up riders."

The driver was nothing to me. I was looking for Grampa Zamp. Still, the guy had not hit me with his pipe. I said, "It must happen sometime."

"The drivers who let it happen no longer work for us."

"Can you tell me where truck number eighty-two went last night after it left the Convention Center?"

She glanced at the computer. Sure. Everything anybody might want to know would be on the old hard disk. Bill could get into their system with less trouble than a drunk would have getting into a can of brewski. Given the chance. This woman didn't seem the type to give it to me, not even if I were at my best. She said, "I don't see why I should."

I nodded casually and said, "No reason, I suppose. Can I use your phone to call Mr. Will's son, Whipper?"

Her plucked eyebrows went up and looked like bows over her eyes. She put down her coffee cup and set her hands flat on the desk. Her nails were long and the color of blood. "You weren't kidding before about meeting Mr. Will?"

"Want me to describe his aftershave?"

"I wouldn't know it," she said, a little haughty, like a woman who'd been accused of using catsup on her steak.

"You still don't trust me. That's fine. Why don't you call Willville and ask for Whipper Will? You probably have the number there someplace."

She glared at me, but didn't say anything as she pulled out a large spiral-bound book. After finding the number she wanted she punched it into the telephone and waited. "Whipper Will, please," she said, and watched me carefully, not wanting to miss the appearance of the first cracks in my composure. I smiled at her. Bill rocked on his heels.

She went through operators and secretaries like Kleenex. At last she said, "Mr. Will? Mr. Whipper Will?" There was a space during which someone could have said yes or no. "One moment, please." Like a challenge, she held out the phone to me.

Bill tried to grab it, but I pushed him aside. With the receiver to my head, I said, "How you be, Holmes?"

"Zoot?"

"Right the first time."

"You have a secretary now?"

"Just temporary. They got Zamp."

"Who got Zamp?"

"Guess."

Whipper breathed at me for a while. Almost whispering, he said, "How did you know I was here?"

"If you're working for your father where else would you be? I was kind of hoping you'd seen the gang."

"That makes two of us."

"I'd like to come out and look around."

"You think my father would make things that simple?"

"He might. If he knew we thought he was too smart to be simple."

Whipper breathed at me some more, probably thinking about scams and double-scams and triple-scams. "Come ahead," he said. "I'll show you around the magnificent Will Industries laboratories."

I handed the phone back to the woman behind the desk. She hung up slowly, without making a noise. Very politely, she said, "I still can't tell you where that truck has been. The truth is, I don't know myself."

I nodded and said, "I'll remember you to the boss."

Bill and I walked out the glass door and got into the Chevy and drove away. I was hot on the trail of something. I hoped it was Zamp.

11

Willville

Willville was inside the southeastern edge of Los Angeles County, so Bill had the place in his bubble memory. The morning was still young, and a lot of traffic was out frolicking in it. My Chevy slid down the Santa Ana Freeway like a barge on a river of mud.

I had not slept well in the car. My muscles were stiff from the cold and felt like bundles of sticks. Also not helping much were unfamiliar noises and nightmares about Zamp, and the fact that I was not really built to sleep sitting up anyway. Not any more than an Earth person. I was more alert than I had been that morning, but I was about as smart as usual.

The air was cool, but I could tell by its hard smell that by afternoon it would be hot. Like love, credulity gas was in the air; it must have been squatting all over the L.A. basin, but except in a few lucky places it was not concentrated enough to matter.

Big trucks crept along like everybody else, grunting in their lower gears like old men mounting stairs. I spotted a few Melt-O-Mobiles, but they were all in use and not making gas. A few cars were driven by androids, but not even they could make headway against the impacted mass of cars.

I sniffed taillights for over an hour, came to my exit at last, and got off the freeway. At the bottom of the ramp was a collection of candy-colored boxes called the Android Motel. Though it was daytime, their neon sign was on. It represented a muscular guy waving at the traffic. He wore little else but a blue collar.

The whole neighborhood was like a carnival that had stayed too long. The atmosphere of the place was silly, and those who traded on it tried to make silliness a virtue. You could not go half a block without running into Android this and Blue Collar that. It was as bad as Hollywood, but newer, cleaner, and somewhat less sanctimonious about its historical importance.

I lined up the Chevy behind a lot of other cars waiting for a chance to use the visitor's entrance to the Willville parking lot. Two dollars were taken from me by a kid who was so wholesome he didn't seem natural. He nearly squeaked when he moved. Maybe he'd been raised in a mayonnaise jar. He wore a striped shirt and white pants that were probably cleaner now than when he'd put them on.

The lot was crowded, but spaces must have been available if you knew where to look. A few times I was just behind the guy who got an empty. The driver was always an android, probably with the superpower of finding places to park. After a while I enjoyed the performance even less.

I said to Bill, "Why can't you find places to park like that?"

"I'm not designed for it. Read the brochure." He surprised me by opening a door in his side and offering me a folded piece of slick paper. I told him to put it away for later, when I didn't have so much on my mind. The disappointment he showed as he put it away was probably just my imagination.

Just when I thought I was going to spend the day exploring the majestic wonders of the parking lot I found a spot and slid into it before an android flew in from San Diego to take it ahead of me. It was nice to know they weren't perfect.

Bill and I rode to the front gate on a white tram, getting curious looks from the driver and the attendants. Paranoia told me they were looking at my nose, but in this place, the fortress of androids, I was pretty sure that Bill was the attraction. Bill didn't notice and I didn't point it out.

The Will name I mentioned did not impress the clean young things at the gate. They probably heard that stuff all the time and had been told to ignore it. I paid admission for two. It was less than the Latvian national debt and not quite as much as a scalped front-seat ticket to a rock concert, but more than a good dinner at a restaurant where they parked your car for you.

Seeing Willville, I knew the sharp businessmen who ran the places outside the park were amateurs. Bill and I walked across a drawbridge of a mighty castle and found ourselves someplace back in Earth's history. The smell of credulity gas was strong enough to build a condo on.

Bill gawked and I could not blame him. He and I stood at the end of a long street that wandered like a river between small well-barbered huts and half-timbered buildings like the peasant cottages and inns in a Robin Hood movie. Crowds broke around us and hurried up the street, ready to believe anything. The castle towered over us with real towers.

Behind us and to one side, over an open archway in one wall of the castle, was a carefully lettered sign that said CASTLE OF ANDROID PROGRESS.

"Cousins," Bill said, and waddled toward the archway.

"Later," I said, and walked up the street. I wasn't here to visit Bill's relatives.

Bill followed while he agreed that later was a great idea.

Willville was a big place and Zamp and the surfers could be anywhere. I didn't know how smart to get. Would Mr. Will hide them in the most obvious place or in the least obvious? In plain sight? I'd outsmarted myself before. Maybe Mr. Will was counting on my doing it now.

I started out checking every hut, but after the first few I lost my taste for plastic shields, rubber spears, arrows with suction-cup tips, and candy in the shape of armored knights—especially armored knights with blue plastic collars. I also did not want a Crusader Cola or a Friar Tuck Burger. I stood outside a hut that sold good-luck charms and watched a cart full of smiling, waving tourists being pulled along by a horse that was in no particular hurry. The horse and the driver each wore a blue plastic collar.

A few times I tried one of the doors between huts that said NO ADMITTANCE. The first time, I was caught by an android dressed as a soldier in chain mail and a shiny metal hat in the shape of a bullet. Gently but firmly he insisted that I return to the public part of the park. Once I actually got through one of those doors and found more security, this time in the form of a woman wearing a gray uniform that made her look lumpy and mannish. She was more suspicious than the guy in the chain mail but just as firm.

I could see now that stumbling around Willville would be pointless. I might find what I was looking for, but more likely I would grow old trying. I needed a clue. It was the one thing not for sale in any of those huts.

Near me, surrounded by a crowd, was an android dressed for the period in dull green tights and a brick red jerkin. His shoes matched his jerkin and curled up at the toes. A jaunty green hat had a long, ridiculous feather in it. At the moment he was playing some kind of pregnant guitar and singing a song about hunting Robin Hood in the forest green-o. When he was done he took off his hat and bowed low to the tourists' applause.

As the guy strolled away strumming his ax, I sidled up to him and said, "I'm looking for the Will Industries Labs."

He gave me a smile that was several centuries out of date and said, "Peradventure, good sirrah, it is yonder, in Victorian London." He pointed up the street with the neck of his instrument. I thanked him and he bowed to me, almost taking my eye out with his feather.

Bill and I walked up the street to a square surrounded by a high box hedge. A sign let down on a chain told me the hedge was the outside wall of the Louis XIV Maze. Shrieks and laughter came from the inside. Bill wanted to go in, but I didn't have time to get lost just for fun. I was confused enough already just doing my job.

Through a gateway of fluted columns was the world of the ancient Greeks and Romans. Opposite, through an arch made by the crossed necks of two rugged dragons hacked from tree trunks, was the world of the Vikings. Over Bill's protests I kept walking and on the far side of the maze came to a wrought-iron gate big enough to let in a chorus line of guys on stilts. In front of it people were just climbing down from one of the carts. The android driver turned a metal wheel not much bigger than a doughnut and leapt from the cart as it began to fizz and evaporate like one of the Melt-O-Mobiles. He rode away on the horse.

On the other side of the iron gate was a brick street lined with gray stone buildings. I don't know how the designers managed it, but the air seemed to be darker and cooler here. Maybe it was just because the buildings seemed to be a little dirty. Horse-drawn cabs bustled by. A crowd of laughing tourists followed a guy dressed like Sherlock Holmes as he ran down the street peering at everything through a large magnifying glass.

"Are we having a good time?" I said to Bill.

"Later?" Bill asked.

"You're right," I said. "It has to get better."

At the far end of the street was a long gray building covered with frozen fountains of fancy carving. A sign told me it was a scaled-down replica of the Houses of Parliament. Evidently Mr. Parliament, whoever he was, liked a little elbow room when he went inside.

The lobby of the replica had nothing to do with Victorian London. It held wide expanses of chrome and glass, which must have saved Mr. Will a bundle on paint. One wall was a montage of photographs, some of them fuzzy with age and having suffered through enlargement. They showed hotels, restaurants, radio and TV stations, a lot full of old business signs, big industrial complexes, big boats, big airplanes. Mr. Will was evidently very big on big. Over it all was a sign that said THE WILL INDUSTRIES FAMILY OF COMPANIES.

I avoided the line for what the advertising called "a fascinating tour through the Super-hero Android plant" and talked to the android guarding the business entrance. She was a comfortable brunette who wore massive amounts of clothing that gave the impression of being a uniform. Her smile was friendly but not ostentatious and was no more a part of her than the badge that said her name was Irma. I told her why I was there. She glanced at Bill, then got on a telephone and had a short whispered conversation. When she finished she used up another smile and told me to take the elevator behind her to the third floor.

The doors opened as we approached, and when we got inside they closed. The third floor button was already lit. The car went up. Mr. Will had me in his pocket now. Yes he did.

12
Ur-Clues

Whipper was wearing his oldest, most faded pair of shorts and a shirt with a pattern so garish, it was less a pattern than a shock treatment. He met Bill and me in a wide, clean corridor that seemed to be made entirely from chrome. Everywhere I looked I saw my own distorted reflection. Eager men and women hurried by wearing clothes that were rather gray and unimaginative next to Whipper's. Many of them wore lab coats or carried clipboards. The really good ones were able to do both at once. A few of them nodded curtly at Whipper as they passed but didn't seem to notice he wasn't wearing the uniform.

That all came to me later. What I noticed first when I stepped from the elevator was the lack of credulity gas in the air. I'd been fighting to ignore the smell for so long, when it wasn't there anymore I almost fell over. The terrible smell had been replaced by cold air that had the flat chemical odor of the inside of a medicine chest.

"What's shakin', dude?" Will said. We shook

hands in the secret surfer way. It's easier to learn than it is to describe, especially if you're drunk enough.

"Not much," I said. "I'm still short one grandfather and any number of surfers. What's shaking with you?"

"Getting Dad's stuff wired is all," he said gayly as he led Bill and me down the hall. We went into an office that was half laboratory. One wall was all windows. A couple of cars could have parked in there, still leaving enough room to hold a tea dance. Bill was fascinated by the glassware set up in long frames. Some liquid dripped and some of it bubbled. Bill didn't know where to look first.

I told him not to touch anything and went to sit on the visitor's side of Whipper's desk—a prairielike expanse now covered with papers. Resting on the computer was a stack of paper plates, the top one of which held a half-gnawed bagel.

"Can we talk?" I said.

Whipper put a finger to his lips and turned on a tape player. The Beach Boys began to sing a song in praise of the surfing life.

Whipper said, "I don't think the room is bugged, but it's a big room." His face lost that eager look and hardened into grim contemplation. "You haven't found them."

"If I had a small army and a couple of weeks I could probably check out Willville. Without the help I'm just fishing without bait."

"Clues?"

"Not that I've noticed. Will you show me around? Something may leap out at me."

Whipper rolled away from his desk and, carrying the tape player, led me and Bill back into the hallway. He slunk along, snapping his fingers to the music. Nobody told him not to. He took me from lab to lab. On the far side of some of them were big windows through which I saw darkness and the vague shapes of tourists, like ghosts watching from another dimension.

Most of the work was done at the cellular level, so all I saw were very serious men and women bent over microscopes. In one room we watched an android with electrodes taped all over his body, even to places where having electrodes might seem a little uncomfortable. A woman turned a dial and the android's body shook, once, twice. I couldn't watch. The android continued to twitch as we left the room.

I stood in the hallway with Whipper and Bill, wishing I had a cigarette. I don't smoke, of course, but if I did this would be the time to do it. Whipper said, "We have to test them."

"Sure you do."

"I passed a test once," Bill said.

I studied Bill just to have something to look at. I'd learned a lot about androids, but was no closer to finding Zamp and Bingo or anybody else than I had been when I'd walked in the gate. I said, "Do you have anything else to show me?"

I must have sounded a little cross because Whipper said, "Look, Zoot, I'm not hiding anything." He snapped his fingers and I could al-

most see the light bulb go on over his head. He
said, "There is something else."

We had not taken more than a step when
Darken Stormy came out of an office, leaving
male laughter behind her. She looked fairly ter-
rific, dressed in a dark blue suit that did nothing to hide the fact she was female. Miles of legs
in sheer stockings that might have been the
same shade of blue ended in spike-heeled pumps
that ticked on the floor as she walked over to
us, lighting her way with a smile. Her lips didn't
really need the red paint, but the color made
them astonishing instead of merely luscious.

"Whipper," she said as if she were greeting
him at her front door. She took one of his hands
in both of hers, cradled it as if it were a fresh
egg, and pulled him close. Her nails matched
her lips, as they would. Her smile hardened for
the moment she glanced at me and said,
"Hello."

The smile warmed up when she looked back
at Whipper. If eyes can have stars in them, she
had stars in hers. Or maybe it was just the fluorescent lighting. Whipper plastered a goofy
smile on his face and said, "Yo, dudette!"

Darken's smile bent a little, but it was still a
nice smile. She said, "I'm so pleased you decided to come back to work for your father."

"It was, like, you know, a gnarly wipeout."

She nodded as if she knew what that meant,
and performed her wind chime laugh. "Oh,
Whipper, I love it when you talk like that." She
rubbed her front against his, maybe trying to

make a fire, and said, "We could meet for a drink after work."

Whipper was doing his best not to react as if he enjoyed being that close to her. I could tell it was a strain. From what I knew about humans it would be a strain for any man who had a full complement of hormones. Still, Darken rubbing against your body was probably better than being stung to death by hornets.

"Not tonight, Darken. I'm really, like, stoked about my research, you know? I'm gonna do some slashing and bashing tonight."

I didn't think it was possible, but Darken made a mistake then. She said, "Don't worry. I won't tell Bingo."

Whipper dropped his composure, but he made a good recovery. He leaned into Darken and, as if he were asking where a good pizza joint might be, said, "You know where Bingo is?"

"Why, no," she said softly. "Don't you?"

He extricated his hand from her grip and said, "Come on, Zoot. I had something to show you."

I tipped my fedora at Darken. Bill wanted to shake her hand, and woodenly, she let him. I pulled him away. She looked after us, stunned as if Whipper had struck her between the eyes with a mallet. I could feel her glaring at us as we walked down the hallway, her glare poking three feet out through my chest.

We rounded a corner and Whipper let out a breath. He said, "Do you think she knows?"

"Do you think it matters?"

He looked at me sharply. Then his face relaxed and he shook his head. "She wouldn't tell if she knew. And I'm not much into torturing women till they talk."

"Still," I said, musing out loud, "it's interesting that she's here, isn't it? She must be more than just a pretty face hired to decorate a trade show."

"How much more?"

I shrugged, a tick I'd learned on Earth. It was possible Mr. Will had hired her, hoping she could convince Whipper to come back to work. It was possible he'd suggested it, and she'd thought it was a good idea. It was even possible that she'd had the idea all on her own and Mr. Will showing up fifteen minutes later was a coincidence. Yes, and it was a coincidence that my great-aunt Hattie ate three pounds of chocolate-covered coffee beans a day and had the same fragile figure as the backside of an elephant. "I don't know," I said. "Guessing might be fun."

"You're talking about my father."

"I'm talking about the man who probably kidnapped your girlfriend, your best bros and my grampa Zamp."

The anger drained out of his face and his mind went somewhere else. I thought maybe he'd forgotten where we were till he turned in at another door. This one was thick and heavy and closed with a shush behind us. Beyond was the biggest room I'd seen yet. The walls, the floor, and even the ceiling were concrete. Pipes of various sizes ran from wall to wall and from floor to ceiling. The room was filled with heat and the hiss of steam. In the center of the room was a round metal vat big enough for water polo. Over the vat, catwalks hung from the ceiling just beneath the pipes. A heavy machine arched over the vat in the pose of a cat investigating a fishbowl. The machine was growling.

As he strolled across the floor, Whipper said, "Not many outside people know this place exists. Fewer have ever been in here."

He turned off the tape player and set it down at the foot of a metal stairway, which he began to climb. Bill and I followed him up and the three of us looked into the vat. At the end of the heavy machine the blades of a beater were sunk nearly to its shaft in grainy brown stuff, which it slowly mixed as it growled.

"Oatmeal," Bill said.

Whipper said, "Pretty close. This is the urmedium. Everything you can order at a fast-food joint is made of this—shakes, burgers, fries, everything. A little food color, a little artificial flavor, a little sculpting, and whammo."

"Whammo," Bill cried. "A Friar Tuck Burger."

I said, "What's it doing here?"

He looked at me and smiled in a secret way appropriate to that room. He was enjoying lifting the veils one at a time. He said, "It's also the stuff that androids are made of."

After watching the beater work for a moment, I said, "Looks a little thin to be walking around."

"We use a solvent to keep it that way. We wouldn't want this stuff, just as it is, to crawl out of the vat and go looking for adventure. When we want to make something we add a chemical that allows it to harden, inject the mixture into a mold, and pretty soon—"

"Whammo," Bill said, pleased to contribute.

Whipper plunged the fist of one hand into the palm of the other, and said "Whammo" again.

"Why keep it a secret?"

Whipper descended the metal stairs one rung at a time and picked up his tape player at the foot of it. He was halfway across the floor before he turned and said, "Will Industries doesn't think it would be good for business if people saw where androids actually come from."

I nodded. "I was in a restaurant kitchen once," I said. "I had been happier before. Maybe Will Industries is right at that."

When we were back in the hall Whipper turned on his music and began to act like a surfer again. We walked in the direction of his office. I said, "Any more places the public doesn't get to see?"

"No clues yet?"

"No even an ur-clue."

"Hi-ya, dudes," Whipper said as a group of his scrubbed co-workers passed. Some of them waved, a little embarrassed.

Instead of taking us back to his office Whipper took us to the elevator. While we waited, Whipper said, "Don't blame me for this."

"Blame you for what?"

"You'll see."

When the elevator came we went to the top floor. Whipper had to punch in a code on the floor buttons before the doors would open.

We came into a place that didn't even know the floors below existed. It was a big room with a fireplace at one end and a picture window at the other. Near the fireplace and under a chandelier that looked like a countess's earring was a wooden table polished to a high gloss and big enough for shuffleboard. The chairs had high narrow backs and were probably more stylish than comfortable. Scattered around the room were small round tables and overstuffed chairs. Wrought-iron candle holders holding candles smaller than harpoons were attached to the white stucco walls. Over the fireplace was a painting of Whipper in short hair and a gray suit; he was with Mr. Will and a woman I had never met. She was not quite beautiful, but her face showed an intelligence and a warmth that in the right circles would take her further than beauty.

As if he'd accidentally stepped on my foot, Whipper said, "I'm sorry, dude."

"Sorry for what?"

He shook his head as he walked to a glass case. Inside was a crystal fishbowl with some crystal fish inside. Light collected there and threw it away. He said, "Look at all this stuff. What kind of person would spend this much money just for a place to live?"

"Somebody who could afford it?" Bill said.

Whipper nodded glumly as he sat in one of the uncomfortable chairs around the big table. "I'm sorry, dude."

"While you're being sorry could you kind of tell me what this place is?"

"Most of the time my father lives here."

I waded across a maroon carpet and tried not to skid on the wide hardwood floor beyond. I leaned against an arched doorway and tried to imagine what might be down the hall. I said, "Can I look around?"

"You think they're here?"

"I think I don't know."

Another voice, a hard voice without pleasure in it, said, "Unless you have a policeman with a search warrant in your pocket you will continue not to know."

I looked in the direction from which the voice had come. Standing with one hand touching the arm of an overstuffed chair was Mr. Iron Will.

13

Progress

He was wearing a suit and tie. In one hand he swirled a potbellied glass that had amber fluid in it. He wore the small potent smile of a man who'd had his suspicions confirmed. He said, "What, exactly, are you looking for?"

"Shit," Whipper said with disgust.

Mr. Will looked at me and said, "Perhaps *you* are speaking in something other than vulgarities today."

"I manage once in a while," I said.

Mr. Will smiled at that.

I said, "We're looking for Whipper's surfer friends and my grandfather. We thought they might be here."

"Why?"

Whipper said his vulgarity again and Mr. Will crinkled his nose.

I said, "You'll be delighted to hear that you are our number one suspect. We can't think of anybody else who would want them."

"Why would *I* want them?" His voice was as flat as the table at the end of the room.

"Well," I said as if explaining when to add the

egg whites, "we figure you're holding the surfers to make sure that Whipper continues to work for you. Maybe you want my grandfather to make sure I stay off your back."

"If that was my object the abduction doesn't seem to have done any good."

"Whipper is here," I said.

"I wasn't aware that he needed the kind of pressure you describe."

"Be aware, dude," Whipper said.

Mr. Will walked across the room and put his glass on the table where it would probably make a ring. That didn't seem to bother him. He said, "I will say this once, and I hope you're listening. I didn't abduct your friends. I have no interest in your friends. If somebody did abduct them, I'm sorry, but I had nothing to do with it. Is that clear enough for you?"

"Is that clear enough for you?" I said to Whipper.

Whipper said a different vulgarity, but it caused the same reaction in Mr. Will as the other one had.

"I will tell you this," Mr. Will said. "I run a nice, smooth operation here. Anybody who buys a ticket is welcome regardless of religion, creed, or belief. Even you, Mr. Marlowe, and your hunk of SSR tin are welcome if you buy a ticket and come in through the front gate. Have a swell time. But if you start poking that impressive nose of yours into my private life again, I'll have a restraining order on you so fast your head will swim."

"I've been warned."

"Good-bye, Mr. Marlowe. Whipper, I believe you have work to do." He watched us as if he expected us to blossom.

Whipper helped me a little when I took him by the elbow and strong-armed him to his feet. "Come on, Bill," I said. I nodded to Mr. Will as we passed, but Whipper looked straight ahead. Whipper pushed a bump in the fancy carving around the elevator, and a moment later the car arrived with a soft musical note.

On our way down Whipper made a sickly smile and said, "That was better than some of the rides."

I said, "You still think your father is not the right kind of guy to get what he wants by holding people for ransom?"

"I wouldn't be here if I still thought that."

"Then I'm pretty much free to do what I have to do."

Whipper frowned and glanced at me sideways. The car stopped at the third floor and we walked out into the chrome corridor. He was so preoccupied with what I'd said, he didn't even bother to walk like a surfer.

I followed him to the door of his office, where he turned to me and said, "Just don't hurt him."

"No more than I have to."

He didn't like that, but it was the best answer I had and he knew it. He nodded and went into his office. Bill and I hurried back to the elevator and rode down to the first floor with a sleek fat man carrying a sample case. He tried to start a conversation with me about the weather; I agreed with everything he said, which seemed to be all he wanted.

At the bottom he wished me a nice day and walked off as if his pants were on fire. I came around to the receptionist and said, "Mr. Will told me to wait for him. He come down yet?"

"Not yet," she said, then bit her lip, thinking maybe she shouldn't have told me that and not knowing why not.

I thanked her and took up a position just outside the entrance where I could see the elevator doors. I knew I could wait for hours, maybe days. He lived up there, after all, and had no reason that I knew of to go out. Except one. I hoped that I had upset him enough that he might want to check on his captives, and that he might want to check on them pretty quick. It was the same impulse that made a man pat his coat pocket after being bumped by a stranger to make sure his wallet was still there.

Sherlock Holmes went by, trailing tourists the way a comet trails stardust. A very official-looking type in a blue hat like the thumb of a glove strolled past twirling his baton. He smiled at me and went on. He was nothing but law, all prettied up for the party, but law nevertheless. If I was still there when he came by again he would probably talk to me.

Mr. Will came out of the elevator like a bull out of a rodeo chute and did not bother to stop at the receptionist's desk. I saw her put up one hand, about to call him, but he stepped along pretty good, and by the time she decided to open her mouth he was gone. I was right behind him.

He marched out of Victorian London and skirted the maze. I was afraid he'd go in, but he didn't. He went between the marble columns and sort of strolled among rides with names like Slideway of Olympus, Ulysses' Boat Ride, and Pegasus's Carousel. He did not have a Hebe Cola or a Minotaur Burger.

He walked just fast enough to make the chase interesting for me but never so fast that Bill and I couldn't follow him with a little work. If he was just a brisk walker I might actually learn something. If he wanted me to follow him I was probably walking into a trap. That was all right. I was ready for a little honesty about now. I hadn't slept in a bed since night before last, and losing Zamp had been a lot of work. My eyes felt like birds' nests and my body was a leather sack full of bones and old rags.

Mr. Will walked down the Robin Hood street. I could keep closer now because of the crowds. He stopped at the entrance to the Castle of Android Progress and looked around. Did he want to make sure I was still following or just the opposite? Satisfied one way or the other, he ducked inside.

"Come on, Bill," I said, "now's your big chance."

"It's later?"

"It won't get any more so."

"Cousins," he cried, and waddled in through the entrance.

Bill and I walked into a dim hallway that pretended to be made of big rocks. The hallway was lit by torches held out from the walls by horizontal arms. The head of each torch was not on fire but held an orange electric flickering. Between the torches were windows through which the customers could view scenes from the history of artificial men. Bill trotted from one to the next, his eyes glowing a little in the semidarkness.

One window showed a big creature made of dirt menacing a guy wearing a small round hat. The plaque said the dirt creature was a golem. We saw Dr. Frankenstein and his monster, and Isaac Asimov inventing the positronic brain. The invention of the android was accompanied by soft pink light and angelic singing. I saw no mention of Mr. Knighten Daise or of Surfing Samurai Robots.

The hallway twisted and curved, as uncertain as a kid choosing an ice-cream flavor. I hustled Bill along pretty fast, but I still lost Mr. Will more than once as he went around a corner.

He disappeared and I pulled Bill away from a window showing the golden Maria robot from *Metropolis* shaking hands with Robby from *Forbidden Planet*. Beyond the corner was a straight corridor lined by androids on pedestals, each of them looking noble and just about to move in the dappled light. The corridor was empty. Unless he'd run faster than a human can run, Mr. Will had not entered it.

To one side was a small room lit by one of

those cockamamy electric torches. There were no windows in this room. No nothing. Just a single flickering torch that made nervous shadows against the smooth stone walls.

There was no place for Mr. Will to hide. He had gone up in nothing, like one of his evaporating cars.

14

Private Parts

I stared at the empty room glumly, knowing what I would have to do next. I didn't want to do it. I was no less tired than I had been when Mr. Will had begun his constitutional across Willville. I felt as if I were wearing a diving suit. I wanted to curl up on the nice soft flagstones and sleep for a day or two.

But that wouldn't find Zamp and the others. And I was convinced that was about to happen. Where better for Mr. Will to hide them than in some secret room in his very own personal castle?

Bill and I stood in a wing of shadow between two show windows and watched the entrance to the side room. Most people passed us as if we weren't there. A lanky woman in white short-shorts and a piece of blue elastic across her top stopped when she saw me. I didn't move. She came closer and, probably thinking I was one of the exhibits, poked me gently in the cheek with one finger. I smiled. She yelped and hurried down the long straight hallway where Mr. Will had not gone.

The entire population of Los Angeles County went by in small groups, goggling at the mechanical wonders. A suspicion grew like a strangling weed that Mr. Will either wasn't coming out or had gone out another way. I was about to risk meeting him on his own turf when I blinked and he was standing at the threshold between the small empty room and the dark corridor. How long had he been there? Had I fallen asleep on my feet?

Mr. Will strolled out the long hall in no hurry—like a man who knew he was important and that other important people would wait for him if they wanted him. I watched him walk out through a fan of sunshine at a doorway at the far end.

Still watching the place where I'd last seen Mr. Will, I ran across the dark corridor with Bill and went into the small bare room, glaring at it as if it had personally done me harm. I said, "We're looking for a way out of here other than the way we came in. One of these stones will probably trip open a door if we tap it or push it just right."

"Tapping and pushing. Got it, Boss," Bill said, but didn't move.

"Start pushing and tapping," I said.

Bill started at one side of the room and I started at the other. I stopped us a few times when paying customers went by, and once, a round-faced kid with a bush of red hair looked around the corner. I told him we were fixing the bricks. He nodded and went away. Nobody else bothered us.

Half an hour later I had put fingerprints on every stone as high as I could reach, and all I had to show for it was calluses on my fingertips and a kink in my neck. Above me was a good two feet of wall that Mr. Will was tall enough to reach.

I would have stood on Bill's shoulders, but he didn't have any, so I had him stand on mine. He did not manage to get aboard the first time. At last I pulled and he jumped at the right moment and landed on my shoulders with the weight of a locomotive. I grunted, then half-turned and propped myself against the wall with both hands.

"Push and tap," I said.

We danced like drunken acrobats all around the room, Bill pushing and tapping, me grunting as we went. When we found nothing, I took Bill around again. Still nothing. We stopped and Bill reached out for the torch to keep his balance.

"It's loose," Bill said, and wobbled it a little.

Of course it was loose. If my brain had been brighter than the underside of a theater seat, shaking the torch would have occurred to me first. I yelled up at him, "Can you work a four-speed stick shift?"

"Sure, Boss. I just can't see over the dashboard."

He thought that was pretty funny, and maybe it was. I had Bill run through the gears with the torch. When he got to third, something in the end wall clicked and a straight floor-to-ceiling crack appeared.

I ordered Bill back to the floor, where he landed with surprising grace and bobbed on his springs. I looked at the opening for a moment, enjoying the feeling of triumph. Then I pushed the door open to see if I deserved to feel it.

The door was perfectly balanced. It fell open at my touch without a squeak. On the other side, three steps descended along a short brown hall-way; at the other end was an intricately carved wooden door that looked as if it had been lib-erated from an old church.

The wall opened from this side with a stan-dard door lever. I made sure it would work for me, and I closed the wall to keep out the riffraff. Bill and I walked down the three steps and I licked my lips before I pulled open the carved wooden door.

I knew what I expected to find: row after row of cages, each containing someone I knew; or all of my friends in a deep pit, or stretched out on instruments of torture, or hanging by their thumbs. I did not expect what I actually found behind that door.

It was a square room that rose in rugged gray stone on four sides to a skylight three or four floors above. In the center of the room, a small fountain chuckled and sparkled into a square pool in which big orange fish swam without care. About half a mile beyond the pool was a wide desk with a high-backed black leather chair behind it. Papers were stacked on long, low tables around the desk. On the wall behind the desk were some framed documents written in fancy script to make them look more important. To one side was a door that was three-quarters shut. It was an office. It was a very nice office, but that's all it was.

I told Bill to stay where he was and without sound I crossed the stone courtyard and looked in at the partly opened door. Inside was a neatly kept bedroom and beyond that a bathroom. This was Mr. Will's retreat. He probably had a freezer full of pizza around somewhere and a microwave oven.

The papers on the long, low tables were business reports of some kind, full of tall columns with big amounts at the bottoms. Even up close the framed documents didn't seem to mean anything.

The desk belonged to a man who did his work elsewhere, or had somebody else do it. On one corner was a rocking horse made of thick silver wire. On another was a statue of an android. A framed photograph stood on the desk where Mr. Will could see it. It showed himself and Whipper and the strong pleasant woman. The drawers of the desk were not locked. One contained a bottle of brewski. Another contained a magazine with pictures of women who seemed happy to mostly not be wearing any clothes and a paperback novel called *Guns of the Pecos*.

In the center of the desk, its edges lined up

with the edges of the blotter, was a single sheet of notepaper under a brass paperweight in the shape of a goldfish. On the paper was a list of names you would definitely want to consider for your next brewski bust. There was the mayor of Los Angeles, the guy who owned the local baseball team, Knighten Daise, Max Toodemax, a woman who hosted an early morning TV show, and a few more. Daise and Toodemax and a few of the others had checkmarks against them. Others did not.

I tried to make something out of this, but I couldn't. A man in Mr. Will's position would want a place where nobody could find him—a private place where he could work, relax, and indulge in his manly vices. As far as the list went, it was not difficult for me to believe that Iron Will would mix with people like this. Maybe he was just throwing a party.

At the top of the desk was a calendar that showed the entire month. The square three days hence was circled in red. In the same red ink it said, "The lab—10:30 A.M."

I used the phone on Mr. Will's desk to call the Willville operator. I asked for Whipper Will. When he came on the line, I asked him if anything important was happening at his lab in three days.

"Not that I know of."

"What about at another lab?"

"Not that I know of."

"Would you know of it if there was?"

"If it was a Will Industries lab, of course. I'm

the big kahuna and the boss's son. Why do you ask?"

"A breeze just went by, that's all. I'll tell you about it when I see you."

I hung up, and while I absentmindedly wiped my fingerprints off the telephone with my handkerchief I wondered if another secret door existed somewhere, maybe back through the bedroom—one that led to the lab. Sure. And another secret door behind that and another behind that. That way lay therapeutic basket weaving and a reserved room with walls done in designer rubber.

"Come on, Bill," I said. "We have a stop to make before we go back to Malibu."

"The excitement *never* stops," said Bill.

"No," I said as I pushed open the wall. "That would make things too easy."

15

He's Only Human

I had a Friar Tuck Burger—a bun like cotton around a thin slab of overcooked meat that I had no trouble imagining had, a short time before, been ur-chemicals. All I tasted was the catsup and onions. The Crusader Cola was better even if it was mostly ice.

Bill and I rode the tram back out into the parking lot, where drivers still circled like vultures looking for a place to stash their heaps. Bill knew right where the car was. Inside it was an oven. We rolled down both windows to let out the hot air and would have waited for the temperature to drop below boiling if it had not been for a Venusian-purple sporty model that was making a lot of noise about wanting the spot.

The drive back to Hollywood was long and I had plenty of time to think. I might as well have concentrated on my driving.

Despite the lack of hard evidence I was still convinced that Iron Will had kidnapped Zamp and the surfers. ID Advertising truck number eighty-two had taken Zamp away and had arrived at ID Advertising about an hour after I had. An hour would have just given the truck time to drop a bundle off at Willville and return to ID Advertising. Of course, there were a lot of places the truck could have dropped Zamp. It was possible the driver had been caught in traffic—it happens even in the middle of the night when Caltrans is out repairing the freeway—and that the time meant nothing at all.

Darken Stormy seemed to hang around an awful lot, but that may have had less to do with a sinister plot than it had to do with her fixation on Whipper. Still, it was obvious from her actions at the trade show that she was working for Mr. Will in a fashion that was more than casual. Darken and Mr. Will were into each other for plenty. But plenty of what?

Something important was happening at a lab at ten-thirty in the morning in three days. The event had something to do with the list on Mr. Will's desk, or not. It had something to do with Zamp and the gang, or not. Or none of it may have had anything to do with anything.

I had clues, all right, but they wouldn't connect. I might as well have kept them rattling around in a shoe box.

It was midafternoon by the time I drove up Franklin Avenue to the Daise Mansion. I spoke to Davenport on the squawk box. He sounded surprised to hear from me, but he let me in through the wrought-iron gates without argument. He came outside to watch me drive up. Something was wrong with his face. I said, "Everything all right?"

He hesitated and said, "It would seem so, sir."

"I didn't know robots had feelings."

Davenport said, "I am a very expensive model, sir," as if that explained everything. His face still looked lopsided.

"Can I come in or will Mr. Daise be joining us here on the steps?"

With a gesture that was nearly human, Davenport nodded and said, "Please come in. Mr. Daise is waiting for you in the library."

Bill and I walked through the hardwood and silence. Davenport knocked on the library door and a voice from inside told the knock to come in. Davenport watched us closely as we entered.

It was the same library with the same dust sifting through the light that fell slanting from the high windows. A man was sitting at the desk at the end of the room, studying a large book through half-glasses. He was dressed in a suit so dark that it made his white shirt seem to be made of neon. His tie had splashes of crimson on it that matched the display handkerchief in his pocket. He was handsome for an Earthman, with crafty eyes and a chin like an anvil. I knew those eyes and that chin from someplace.

The man looked up and in a practiced voice of command said, "Come in, Marlowe. Have a drink." He swept his hand at a silver tray that held a square brown bottle and three glasses, one of them half full.

I said, "I thought Mr. Daise was in here."

The man made a big, enthusiastic laugh that reddened his face and shook the room before it crashed into a hacking cough. The man sputtered as he put the cough out in his drink. He glanced at me as he wiped his face with his handkerchief and almost started to laugh again. Instead he said, "What's the matter, Marlowe? Don't you recognize me?"

I didn't recognize him, but I did recognize the family resemblance to his daughter. The eyes. The chin. Bill sat in a leather wing chair and swung his legs while I approached the desk. I said, "The first time I saw you, you looked like a lobster. A few days ago you looked like a camel. It's kind of a shock to see you with only two legs and wearing clothes."

"I got tired of playing games."

"And now?"

He sipped his drink and gently closed his book as if it were made of eggshells. "*You* asked to see me, I recall."

I had, but now I wasn't sure I should ask him the questions I had in mind. Davenport's face wasn't the only thing lopsided at the Daise mansion today. Mr. Daise's new appearance was part of it, but something else was wrong too. After thinking all that, I just barreled right ahead. Casually, just discussing the weather, like, I said, "I understand you're meeting with Mr. Will in a few days at the lab."

"You understand how?"

"That's confidential. So far."

"It doesn't matter," Mr. Daise said generously. "I don't know anything about such a meeting."

"Or about the lab?"

"No."

"You do remember Mr. Will, don't you? You had him followed."

He frowned at that, working it out. Then he smiled and said, "Of course I remember him. We're going into business together."

He might as well have shot me in both knees. I felt for the chair behind me and sat down hard. His expression never changed while I gripped the arms and caught my breath and tried to understand what he'd just said. I sniffed the air. No credulity gas was in it. I would have smelled it when I came in if there were. But I sniffed just the same. A little stupidly, I said, "You and Iron Will are going into business together?"

He got very enthusiastic, like a kid talking about his paper route. "Not actually together, but we've made an agreement. Surfing Samurai Robots is no longer going to make their top-of-the-line models. Androids are so much more practical. But keep it to yourself till tomorrow, after I make the announcement." He winked at me. We were just two tycoons in gravy up to our chins.

To assure myself that the Mr. Daise before me was nothing like the Mr. Daise I'd met anytime before, I said, "What about the credulity gas?"

"What about it?"

"Last I heard, it was a crime against man, God, and nature."

"Something in the smog." He winked at me again. "And lucky for us. It's good for business."

I nodded, trying to stay calm, and said, "Anything else new?"

"I don't follow."

I stood up and said, "Mr. Daise, it's been a pleasure talking to you. Always an education."

"Come again anytime," he called after me, and started to laugh again.

I grabbed Bill on the way out and closed the door gently behind us. Davenport was waiting. He would have wrung his hands if he'd been programmed for it.

I said, "How long has he been like that?"

"A few days. No more."

"How did it happen?"

"I don't quite know, sir. A limousine pulling a horse-trailer picked him up. When he came back a few hours later, he was as you see him."

"Come on, Davenport, don't make me pull teeth. Who owns the limo? Where did it take him?"

"Mr. Daise didn't say. Can you help him, sir?"

I thought about Zamp and Whipper and the surfers and how much I'd helped *them*. I said, "It's very near the top of my list, Davenport. Very near."

We nodded at each other like a couple of Japanese wrestlers, and he let me and Bill out the door. As my Belvedere rolled down the long driveway, I thought about all the clues Mr. Daise had probably handed me during our conversation. I threw them into my shoe box, where they rattled around with everything else.

An hour later, when I got back to the empty house in Malibu, a car was parked on the cement apron in front of the garage.

16

A Lot of Vacancies

The car was boxy and a noxious green that is used nowhere else but in public buildings. It belonged to Irv Doewanit. I liked Irv, but I also hadn't slept in a bed in a couple of days, and I hadn't heard any straight answers in almost that long. I needed a bath. And because the Friar Tuck Burger had been less like food than any other food I'd ever eaten, I needed a hot meal. All in all, I did not feel like the perfect host.

Doewanit was sitting on the front step reading a newspaper. Maybe it was the same one he'd been reading while watching Mr. Will what seemed like years before. He looked up at me and smiled. I wanted to kick him for looking so healthy and rested but instead I grunted, "Hello, Irv."

"Marlowe, Marlowe," he said as he stood up. "Just the man I wanted to see."

"Take a good look," I said. "I'm fading fast." I stumbled past him to unlock the door. The house was not just empty, it was a dead thing, its soul gone. All the smells in it were old and had lost the edge that even a good smell has when it's new. I listened to the silence until I could hear Doewanit breathing behind me.

"Sit down," I said as I walked into the kitchen. Doewanit had shown me a good time at his place; I would show him a good time here, even if it was a little gray and I couldn't hold it very steady.

A note was stuck to the refrigerator under a magnetic kitchen surfboard. The note had been written by Whipper before he'd left and it told me that tonight was the night of the neighborhood meeting. I cannot tell you how much I did not want to go to that meeting. But I'd promised Whipper I'd go. Besides, Max Toodemax was on Mr. Will's list. Maybe going to the meeting would help me find Zamp. I doubted it. But at the moment I'd doubt gravity.

I found nothing in the refrigerator but a six-pack of brewski and an onion growing a green topknot. I returned to the living room with one of the cans and threw it in Doewanit's direction. He caught it in one hand and opened it and poured some of it down his throat, making his voice box bob.

The phone rang, sounding unnaturally loud. I considered letting it ring, but finally couldn't leave it alone. At the other end was Whipper. In a flat voice, he said, "I found it."

"Found what?"

"The answer. The way to prevent androids from going stale. You just add the same preservatives that are in junk food snack cakes.

Neat, huh?'' The information should have pleased him, but it didn't.

"That's bitchen," I said, relieved. "I guess that means I no longer have a case because everybody's coming home." Whipper could go to the meeting instead of me. I could get some sleep and then take Zamp back to T'toom. We'd both had enough excitement. I was so busy with my fantasy I had to ask Whipper to repeat what he'd just said.

"I said Dad isn't playing it that way. He still won't let anybody go."

"Why not?"

"I guess he likes me working for him." Whipper spit the words at me.

"What about Zamp?"

"Dad won't let *anybody* go. He still claims not to have them."

I felt empty and even more tired than when I'd come in. Behind my eyes I saw eight plastic garbage bags, each the large economy size, each weighted so it would sink to the bottom of the bay. In each was the body of somebody I knew—seven surfers and my Grampa Zamp. I didn't know for sure they were dead. Maybe Mr. Will just liked their company. I supposed it was even possible that he didn't have them. But the nasty thought that he wouldn't let them go because they were already gone wouldn't stay quiet.

"You there, Zoot?" Whipper said.

"Yeah," I said.

"Still on the case?"

"Sure," I said, jolly as a plastic tiara. "I'll find them."

"Let me know. I never liked it here. I like it less now."

We kidded each other for a few more minutes and then hung up. I stood by the phone for a while. Then Doewanit burped politely and I remembered that I'd left him drinking in the living room. I wished he'd done his drinking at home.

I sat down on the couch across the room from him and waited.

He said, "Every little thing all right?"

"Let's say that it is."

He shook his head. "Marlowe, Marlowe, don't be so paranoid. If somebody from Malibu looked the way you look, he'd be in bad shape."

I nodded. If there was going to be any patter this afternoon, it would have to come from him. He took another swig and then rested the can on the arm of the chair. He looked around with a self-satisfied smile.

"I'm kind of busy right now," I said, and stood up. "If you want to finish that brewski, be my guest. There's more in the fridge. Just lock the door behind you on the way out."

He winked at me as if I'd confided in him and said, "Look, I didn't come all this way just to keep you up and drink your beer."

I sat down. It was either that or fall over. I adjusted my face into what I hoped was an interested expression. It probably looked like mashed potatoes.

"Marlowe, Marlowe, we detectives have to stick together, don't we?"

I was about ready to scream at him when he went on.

"A woman from Superhero Androids is after me."

If I'd had ears they would have pricked up then. As it was I leaned forward, the tiredness draining out of me like dirty motor oil.

"Good, Marlowe. You're interested. But I digress. The woman's name is Fran Ignatio and she works in the SA acquisitions department."

"What does she acquire?"

"At the moment, she wants to acquire some cells from my body."

"Kinky."

Doewanit laughed and then said, "Not so kinky. She wants to use the cells to grow an android with my looks and talents for their *Great Detectives* series."

I shook my head and said, "I guess I really am tired. She wants to do *what* with your cells?"

He got very serious all of a sudden and said, "You know that androids are all grown from seed cells that come from donors who have the looks and talents SA wants to push."

"I didn't know that." And I wondered why Whipper hadn't told me. Had he just not thought of it, or was something else going on? Like father, like son? Maybe I didn't know Whipper as well as I thought I did.

But Whipper Will didn't worry me. He was

my friend or he wasn't. If he wasn't he could not hurt me any more than his father had already done. What did worry me was this seed cells angle. Mr. Will could make a copy of anybody he wanted to. Unpleasant possibilities bore down on me like a platoon of tanks.

Then another thought came to me, arriving on a broomstick, black rags fluttering around it. Maybe it came to me because it was unpleasant too. Maybe the idea flew in because Whipper Will and Doewanit had just given me some things to think about. Maybe I knew why Mr. Will had kidnapped Zamp and the surfers. They were worse than dead. They were experiments.

Mr. Will had been astonished when neither Zamp nor I nor any of the surfers was conked by the credulity gas. It had really astonished him bad. If he was keeping them despite the fact he'd gotten what he said he wanted from his son, was it such a long leap that he was keeping them to find out why they didn't react to his poison? On the other hand, maybe I was being optimistic.

But that was all *my* business. It had nothing to do with Irv Doewanit, who so far was only something to step over on the way to bed. He was still drinking and looking around the room as if he were thinking of buying it and was deciding in his mind what color he would like on the walls. I said, "So, you want to stay here."

"Your perspicacity never ceases to amaze me. What do you say?"

Was *perspicacity* another word for nose? I

said, "Why not? We have a vacancy at the moment. We have a lot of vacancies."

"You are a prince among men. I almost hesitate to ask you one more favor."

"Almost," I said, and bobbed my head until I stopped myself.

"You're a detective. I'm a detective. What say you do me a professional favor and get this Fran Ignatio off my back?"

"What do you expect me to do, use a crowbar?"

"You'll think of something. You're that kind of guy."

"I'm working at the moment. I can't tell if it's a case or a couple of cases. I'll take care of your problem when I have the time."

"That's all I ask."

"Meanwhile, you can stay here."

He leapt to his feet, clutched me by both shoulders, and just barely fought the impulse to kiss me on both cheeks like a movie Frenchman. He ran out to his car to get baggage.

I went into the bedroom to take off my hat and coat. I tried to decide if I wanted to eat first or sleep first. But I might as well have tried to pick up a raw egg with chopsticks. I fell asleep deciding.

17

Meet Max Toodemax

Pale yellow light was coming through the curtains when I woke up. I lay on the bed for a while listening to the surf beat at the beach, making a sound like faraway cannons. I let the sound smother me and I feel asleep again.

When I awoke for the second time Bill was watching me from a corner of the dark room, his eyes glowing. Somewhere in the house a fresh pizza roamed. I got up and followed the odor to the living room. Doewanit was sitting on the floor eating pizza from a white cardboard box while he watched a black-and-white movie on television. I asked him to save some of the pizza for me and I went to wash.

Half an hour later I was clean and dressed and full of food. If I'd been human before, I would have felt human again. As it was, I felt like more than a match for five of what I'd been that afternoon.

"You want to come to the neighborhood meeting?" I asked. "We're going to throw out the monarchy."

He was engrossed in a scene in which two

guys were riding across the desert on horses. He waved at me without turning around and said, "Have a good time."

Bill lit the way with his eyes while we walked to the recreation hall where the meeting was to be held. The air was warm and sweet as the breath of a baker's oven, so a lot of people were out that night. A couple of them on roller skates almost knocked me down.

The hall was a small brick building normally used for Cub Scout meetings and senior citizen dances. It was lit by a few poles out in front. The parking lot was filling up fast. Among the real cars, Melt-O-Mobiles fizzed and disappeared. People arrived in their formal T-shirts. Some even wore pants that went all the way to their ankles. They mixed outside like the inmates of a disturbed anthill, talking and making bloody oaths to each other. I would not have wanted to be Max Toodemax that evening.

While Bill watched gnats orbit the white glass ball atop one of the light poles, I wandered into the room and was handed an agenda by a woman sitting behind a card table at the door. She asked for a donation and I gave her a few bucks. Whipper would have wanted it that way.

The room was brightly lit by tubes in the high ceiling. Despite it being only half-filled, and with all the doors open, the room was warm enough to raise a sweat on the humans who were in it. I returned some serious nods. A lectern and a microphone stood on a small stage.

I wandered back outside and stood where I

could watch people walk up from the parking lot. I would have asked Bill to watch with me, but I didn't know myself what I was watching for, so I couldn't tell him.

The crowd got bigger, and not uglier exactly, but tenser, as if the people were waiting for a hanging. Almost nobody went into the hot rec hall. Another car pulled up. It was big and the color of sea foam at night, but it was just another car. I'd been leaning against a low brick wall. I stood up straight now, ready to jump in any direction I had to. Four bruisers got out of the car and almost immediately I smelled credulity gas. Though they were dressed in gray suits and ties I knew the four were androids because of the line of blue plastic that showed just above their shirt collars.

Suddenly I had a funny idea. What if Carla DeWilde could not find a connection between credulity gas and androids and Melt-O-Mobiles because she was doing the experiment all wrong? What if she was missing a third ingredient in the credulity gas, something found outside but not in the controlled environment of her laboratory? Smog, for example. My funny idea might never grow up to be anything more, but Carla DeWilde would want to give it a chance.

The last person out of the car was a man who was taller than his androids. He had short blond hair that looked like a neatly clipped plot of dry yellow grass. His face was long and had sharp bones behind it. Ice-water eyes looked around.

His big workman's hands came up to touch the knot of his pale blue tie. He wore a white sport coat and pants as gray as mouse fur. Shoes were black and highly polished.

Nobody was paying any attention to him. I strolled over and put out my hand. "Mr. Toodemax?" I said.

The androids closed in, and he looked at me. The cold eyes were the color of the bottom of a tin washtub and they did not blink. He said, "Yes?"

"I just wanted to say hello. I'll be at the lab with Mr. Will day after tomorrow."

He said, "You don't look like the kind of person who Mr. Will would employ."

He was right, of course, but the air was heavy with credulity gas. He would believe anything I told him. I said, "Yes I am. I am just the sort of person he would hire. But he forgot to tell me where the lab is. It's a good idea for *you* to tell me."

"I know nothing about a lab." He looked beyond me. I don't know what he saw but it drew his mouth into a straight line.

"Mr. Will wants you to tell me."

He spread his hands and said, "Look, mister. I expected to be harangued tonight. I guess that's why I'm here. But this wasn't the subject. Understand?"

"Sure. I've talked to tough guys before." My confidence was all bluff. Mr. Toodemax frightened me, and not just because he was bigger than I was.

"Tough can be arranged," he said, as sinister as if he'd been wearing a black caul.

"Sorry," I said. "I thought you were somebody else." I stepped aside and let him pass. A crowd stood around us. Nobody in it said a word. I'd seen faces like theirs on hood ornaments. Mr. Toodemax had been looking at the crowd over my shoulder. Now it opened an aisle and Mr. Toodemax used it to get into the rec hall.

I followed the crowd into the building and stood near a door with Bill beside me. I only half-listened to the meeting. Because of the credulity gas, Mr. Toodemax was having an easy time explaining why he wanted to plow the houses under and plant condos. People who'd been wanting his skin tacked on a wall now nodded and smiled.

The part of my brain that wasn't listening to the meeting was working hard on the conversation I'd had with Max Toodemax. I threw another idea into my shoe box and the other ideas slid into place all around it. I didn't know where Zamp and the others were yet, but I knew what Mr. Will's game was. If I could stop him I could save everybody, including these folks having the meeting. If I couldn't stop him, nothing mattered. Not who lived where, or even whether I saved anybody. We'd all be picking grit out of our teeth. Those who had teeth.

The meeting was dull, and, given the credulity gas, predictable. I backed out of the warm room with Bill and strolled toward Whipper's house. The air seemed cooler now, but maybe I'd just gotten used to the heavy warmth in the rec hall.

The night was beautiful, and I could even see a few stars floating over the ocean like angels. Far out on the water, one of the stars could have been a boat. The rec hall was far behind me along with the credulity gas, and I had another few blocks to walk. At the moment, I was passing a lot of closed stores that during the day sold food or souvenirs or clothes. They were as gray and cold as tinsel in a dustbin.

Somebody grumbled into the right side of my head, "You and your bot walk down toward the water, jaunty-jolly, you know what I mean?" He stuck something into my ribs for emphasis. I didn't think it was his finger.

As I walked toward the ghostly surf I chanced a glance over my shoulder. Prodding me and Bill along were all four of Max Toodemax's androids. They were not holding carrots.

18

Home Is Where the Murder Is

Escaping would be too easy if all I had to do was tell Bill to whoop as loud as he could, but I tried it anyway. He whooped and nearly froze the ocean with the noise but the four androids kept walking. Earplugs. They had learned their lesson well.

Pretty soon we would be on the hard sand down by the water and everybody's footing would be more secure. I turned before we got there and held my open hands to my sides, showing I wasn't heeled. Good old Bill, standing next to me, did the same. "Hang on!" I said quietly against the thunder of the breaking waves. The androids couldn't hear me. I was betting they couldn't read lips.

I grabbed Bill by the wrist and swung him at the nearest android, knocking him down. At the end of Bill's arc I let go and he flew off. While the other three, automatically and without thinking, were watching Bill fly through the air, I climbed the first android, grabbing his blue plastic collar on the way to the top. I leapt from the top of his head and was on the other three before Bill hit the sand, knocking them one into the other. They would be confused for less than a second. In that time, I plucked their collars one-two-three.

The four androids lay unmoving in the sand. I sat on the chest of one of them, breathing hard. The whole evening's entertainment had taken maybe three seconds, but my body would be hollering about it for weeks.

"You OK, Bill?" I called.

Bill pulled his head out of the sand. A small whirring motor began inside him and sand sprayed from his mouth in a plume. The whirring stopped and as he walked toward me, he said, "I let go, Boss."

"Don't worry about it, Bill. You did good."

"I do good work."

I agreed with him. I dropped the blue plastic collars near the bodies and walked down to the hard wet sand. The waves curled and fell with crashes, then sneaked up onto the land. Bill trotted next to me on my other side and we went home.

Breathing was still my major concern. While I did it, I wondered if I would ever be safe again. Androids were everywhere, and all of them were made by SA. I'd never know which one had been ordered to kill me till I found out the final permanent way.

Evidently somebody had gotten tired of my snooping around. Whether it was Whipper's father—who less and less looked like a saint—or Mr. Toodemax, or somebody else, they would keep trying to off me until they got the job done right. Of course, I could stop snooping, but that didn't seem like much fun.

By the time I got back to the house I was breathing normally and I'd stopped thinking about Mr. Toodemax and his goons altogether. There was no point scaring myself. I had a job to do. Sure. I'd stopped thinking about them. Stand in the corner and don't think about strawberry yoyogurt.

I opened the door and heard the TV. I walked through the living room, didn't see Doewanit, and assumed he was in the bathroom. In the kitchen, Bill sat on the sink counter while I made a phone call. "Got the number of De-Wilde's Bunch?"

Bill gave it to me and I dialed. After three rings an answering machine came on the line and told me what business hours were. The machine graciously offered to take a message. At the beep I said, "This is Zoot Marlowe leaving a message for Carla DeWilde. I was there a few days ago with Whipper Will asking impertinent questions about credulity gas. I have a theory you might want to test. Try mixing Melt-O-Mobile gas and android cooties with outside air and see what you get. Let me know." I hung up, suddenly wondering who besides Carla De-Wilde would hear that message and if it was just another nail in my coffin. Then I decided it didn't matter.

I considered calling Mr. Daise about my cre-dulity gas theory, but in his present form I didn't think he'd appreciate the information. I'd liked him better as a camel. A lobster, even.

I hoped that Doewanit was still in the mood to watch TV. I still wanted to find Zamp and the others but I had no idea how to continue. Stopping Mr. Will seemed even more unlikely. Watching TV would give me an excuse to sit in one place and not think about anything.

I went back into the living room and the TV was showing somebody in diving gear making a lot of bubbles. Then I saw him. I hadn't seen him from the kitchen because of the couch. I didn't want to see him now, not the way he was.

Irv Doewanit lay faceup on the floor with a look of strangulated terror on his face. His mouth and eyes were wide open, his bow tie was askew. His clothes—what was left of them—looking like shredded wheat. His hair was too stiff to be mussed, but it was mashed down, as if somebody'd sat on it. His face was scratched with bloody parallel lines, over and over until not much of that face was left. His limbs were twisted in unnatural ways, in ways that would be painful if he weren't beyond pain. Some big animal had killed him. Some big animal like a saber-toothed tiger. An android.

I looked at him for a long time. I got up to turn off the television, then went back to look at him again. Irv Doewanit had been a nice guy who wanted nothing more than to walk the walk. He'd purposely turned his back on a million-dollar job so that he could solve crimes out of a ratty little hole of an office in Hollywood, like Philip Marlowe. He should have stayed where he was. Maybe we all should have. I saw again the surprise on the android's face when I'd swung Bill at him. No android would fall for that again.

Onc of Duewanit's hands was open but the other clenched something. I pried the fist open and found a tip of wood painted blue. It might have meant nothing at all but I knew what the thing was—the tip of the wave on the back of the "Surf City" music box Darken Stormy had given to Whipper Will, the little keepsake she'd been so attracted to.

The music box wasn't on the mantel. I looked for it all over the room, starting with the fireplace, which held nothing but the curled brown breakfast-food remains of last winter's fire. The surfers were not the neatest people I knew, so I found a lot of things that didn't matter: stuff like half-sandwiches that were so old the bread was like a layer of sponge and the filling was now dried slime, as tempting as old snot; like crumbling brown newspapers; like bobby pins and pencil stubs and change.

I didn't find the music box anywhere in the living room, so I started on the rest of the house. I got Bill to help me. He was fast and efficient, but didn't have my passion. I worked quickly with the viciousness of a man not really looking but just tearing things apart because he's angry and there's nothing else to do.

I turned up things that had been undisturbed for years and no longer had names. That and

tons of dust I got hot and tired sneezing at. I
found no music box. It wasn't there. If it had
been there, I'd have found it. I had to assume
that or go even more crazy. Irv had not just
grabbed the music box as it fell. Somebody had
taken it, probably after a struggle.

A little wild-eyed, I went back into the living
room and dropped onto the couch. I could hear
Bill in one of the bedrooms moving things
around. I'd been all through that room and I
didn't think he'd find anything. I looked at Irv
Doewanit lying silently on the floor. You're
never that silent in life, not even when you're
sleeping, not even when you're sick. He was too
silent to be good company.

While Bill and I were at the tenants' meeting
somebody or somebody and his friends had
come here with at least one saber-toothed tiger.
This somebody had come here either for the ex-
press purpose of killing Irv Doewanit—in which
case the fact the music box was missing was
just a blind—or to get the music box itself—in
which case the murder of Irv Doewanit was in-
cidental. His only crime was that he'd been
home.

Murdered for a music box. Irv might like that.
It was good enough for a *Charlie Sundown* episode.

I didn't know of anybody who was after Irv
except Fran Ignatio of SA, and she probably was
not the type to commit murder or even have it
done. If she acquired cell donations for the
company she was probably just hired help. SA

couldn't murder everybody that turned them down. It must happen all the time. Word would get around.

Therefore, either Irv had enemies he hadn't spoken about—not even during that one drunken night—or my one and only suspect was Darken Stormy. Nobody else would kill to get a cheap, not very pretty music box. Unless there was something about the music box I didn't know, which was certainly possible but unlikely.

Irv Doewanit had not exactly been a good friend, but we had been pleasantly acquainted, and he had come here seeking sanctuary. I owed him something. Because he'd asked for help, and because in dying in this terrible way he'd given me a certain amount of leverage against Darken Stormy. Even if she hadn't murdered Irv or ordered it done, she might see the logic hin the police thinking she had. If I could prove otherwise, that might be worth something to her, something like the present location of Zamp and the surfers.

I stared at Irv again and said out loud, "I wish you were here, Irv. I'd like to talk this over with somebody." Irv didn't answer me.

I went into the kitchen, punched a number, and got the night operator out at Willville. In a frayed voice I said, "I'd like to speak with Whipper Will."

A woman who sounded as if I'd just awakened her said, "I'm sorry, sir. I'm not authorized to give out that information."

Sounding a little more angry than I wanted

to, I said, "Look, I don't want the combination to the safe. Just connect me. Tell him it's Zoot Marlowe and see if he'll talk to me."

Without saying anything she went away leaving me with relentlessly jolly music. I tried not to think about this evening again, but it kept coming back to me like a nightmare or a greasy dinner. The music went back to the bird cage where that kind of music goes and a phone began to ring. After half a ring Whipper answered it. He asked where I was and I told him.

"Any progress?" he said.

I glanced in the direction of the living room floor and said, "I have a lead. It's kind of complicated. Tell me about that 'Surf City' music box Darken Stormy gave you."

"Just a music box."

"Could it be some kind of collector's item?"

"Maybe. But only if you're a very desperate kind of collector."

"Why keep it?"

Silence hung at his end. I couldn't even hear him breathing. He said, "Tell all, Zoot. You didn't call in the middle of the night just to question my preference in souvenirs."

Whipper was good at keeping secrets. Mine, his, I didn't know who else's. I told him what I'd found when I came home. It was his house. He ought to know anyway.

More silence came from his end, then a single inhalation of breath, and then he spoke in a voice that was calm and solid as an old tree. He said, "As far as I know, it was just a music box, made out of wood and having a cheap Swiss movement. I kept it because Darken and I used to be a hot item and even after we cooled off I still liked her well enough to want to be reminded of her occasionally."

"Bingo must have enjoyed that."

"She didn't mind. She has old boyfriends too. They mean as much as old King Tut."

"We're losing the point here. Can you think of anybody but Darken who might want that music box?"

"No."

"Then I'll have to talk with her. Do you have her address and phone number?"

"Wait a minute." He went away across rugs and hardwood floors. A TV set played. Far off a door closed. Then he came back and gave me an address and phone number he assured me were in Los Angeles County. I told him thanks.

Tensely, he said, "You think she killed him?"

"Her or a friend. Mr. Will can afford good friends."

"My father isn't a murderer."

"You're probably right. Thanks again." I hung up in his face. Whipper was Iron Will's son and it was expected he would try to put the best light on anything his father did. I didn't have that problem.

I told Bill to remember Darken Stormy's address and phone number, then called her. When she answered I pushed down the plunger, hanging up. I should have known she'd be home. It was late. She had to work the next day. But I didn't really want to talk to her yet. I had other things to do first.

I took my finger off the plunger and got a dial tone. I took a deep breath, and dialed 911. When an eager young voice came on the line I said, "I want to report a murder. Sergeant Preston will want to know about it."

The voice took some information from me, and I hung up. I sat down in the kitchen to wait. The living room was a little crowded.

Somebody knocked at the front door, but it was too soon for the police. Besides, they would have arrived with a blast of sirens and a knocking like a rain of bowling balls. This was a tap-tap-tapping from the other end of the world. At first I hadn't even been sure I'd heard it.

I met Bill in the hallway walking in my direction. He said, "Nothing, Boss."

"You still do good work, Bill."

"Yeah."

I took a big chance and opened the door. You never knew who'd be knocking late at night. Deadly androids, friends needing money or a place to stay. Anything. I opened the door. Standing there on the mat, smiling shyly, was Grampa Zamp.

19

Alone Again Again

To say that I had not been expecting Zamp was to say that Custer had not been expecting Indians. I'm afraid I gaped.

Zamp said, "Can I come in?" He seemed to be enjoying my surprise, which he would, so that was all right. Little else about him made sense. He was dressed in flowered walking shorts and a maroon turtlenecked sweater. He'd been wearing the shorts when the androids dragged him away from the Convention Center, but I had never before seen the turtlenecked sweater.

Just to see what would happen, I said, "Good. You're here."

He looked puzzled, then laughed and came in. I led him to the kitchen. On the way he saw Irv Doewanit. His eyes got very large and he said, "I know trouble is your business, but I didn't know you took your work home."

"It happens in the best places. Know him?"

"No. Should I?"

I shook my head. This was getting me nowhere. I said, "So, where have you been?" He stood looking at Irv Doewanit's body as if it were a fish pond.

"It's a long story. I've been around. You know?"

Old Irv made me nervous. I walked into the kitchen and sat in one of the chairs. Bill and Zamp followed. When we were all cozy, I said, "I have plenty of time. How did you escape?"

"Got a brewski?" Zamp said.

I got him one. He opened it and took a sip. He put the can aside and studied me.

I said, "It must be one swell story. I'm waiting to hear it. 'Zamp's daring escape from the clutches of evil.'"

He nodded and said, "Come on. I want to show you something."

He led me back through the living room and then paused to let me go first through the hall. I went first. A moment later, his hands were around my throat and squeezing hard. I backed into him and crushed him against the wall. He made an involuntary "Oof!" and his hands loosened briefly. I turned, brought my hands up between his arms, and knocked them aside. In his eyes was the madness of a rabid dog. "Don't you recognize your old Grampa Zamp?" he said, and laughed, reminding me of jungle documentaries I'd seen on PBS.

I let him come at me. He got his hands around my throat again but this time, instead of knocking his hands away, I went after the blue plastic collar I knew was hidden inside that sweater. He snapped at me and got a grip on me with his mouth. I ignored the needles of pain shooting up my wrist and probed down into the turtleneck. A second later I had a broken blue plastic collar in my hand and the Zamp android was a heap on the floor. Lying there like that, it was difficult for me to believe it wasn't Zamp just sleeping.

I put the collar into my pocket and hauled the android into the hall closet, where I dumped him in among the coats. I turned the lock. I knew it wasn't necessary, but locking that door made me feel better.

Sending that Zamp android had been a nasty trick, and it had been the wrong thing to do. It had momentarily given me joy and unreasonable hope. With those things gone all I had left was anger. That would carry me. Whether Iron Will or somebody else had done this to me, I would find him and stop his clock.

My, my. Such melodramatic threats.

Bill stood at the living-room end of the hallway and said, "That was great, Boss."

"Not bad." I gently rubbed the lipmarks on my wrist.

Sirens came closer and soon were in my lap. Someone politely but definitely knocked at the door and a voice heavy as a sack full of gravel said, "Open up. It's the police." Always the same line. But what other line was there?

I opened the door for a big uniformed cop with a red face. A plastic bar on his pocket said FAVERE. Just behind him was another cop who was smaller and thinner and younger. They were both grim. Favere said, "You're the one who called nine-one-one?"

"Guilty," I said. "Come on in."

He gave me a small polite smile just in the interest of public relations. He and the young cop left the door open so we could hear the police calls and see the red light sweep across the hallway like a lighthouse in Hell. The officers followed me back to the living room, where I didn't have to point out the body. They studied it as if appraising golf balls on a green.

"You touch anything?" Favere said.

"Probably. I didn't see him 'till I'd been home awhile."

Favere grunted and knelt but still didn't touch the body.

Sergeant Preston came in then, still wearing a brown suit and a brown fedora. His trench coat must have been in the car. He was with a neat older man who carried a doctor's bag and wore a small gray mustache. Sergeant Preston and I nodded at each other while the man with the bag went to work on the body. The two uniformed cops looked around, began dusting for fingerprints, and used tweezers to put bits of nothing at all into labeled plastic bags. Bill toddled around after them.

Sergeant Preston sat in the chair he'd sat in a few days before and took out a small notebook. He said, "Things seem to happen to you."

"Things I could do without."

He didn't even swing at that one, but said, "You getting anywhere on the kidnapping?"

"Not anywhere you'd want to go."

"That means no?"

"Yes."

"Try saying no next time. I'm as much a Chandler fan as you are, but I try to have a life too."

"I like your outfit," I said.

He smiled in an aw-shucks way and said, "All right. It's been nice dancing with you, but all right. Your bot have this all down on tape?" He waved the pencil at the body and at the house.

"Not this time. He was with me."

"Talk to me," Sergeant Preston said, and poised his pencil.

I told him I'd been out and where I'd been out to. I told him I'd come back and found the body. It was a dull story but blessedly short. I left out the part about the four android goons and the tip of the music-box wave and the android Zamp. The androids didn't seem to have anything to do with Doewanit's death. I didn't tell about the music box because I had a vague idea: Darken Stormy didn't need my protection and probably didn't want it. But I wanted to speak with her before the police rolled her up in law and put her where I couldn't reach her without a lawyer and a step stool.

When I stopped talking, Sergeant Preston let there be a long space in the conversation during which I heard the clatter of police calls and the insect sounds of the policemen as they moved carefully through the house. While we had been talking a couple of big guys had taken Irv Doe-

wanit away in a bag, leaving only a chalk out-
line to show he'd ever existed. I tried hard not
to let it depress me that a man's life had collapsed in on itself until you could play hop-
scotch with it. I tried and failed.

Sergeant Preston said, "Any ideas?"

"Aside from the usual nasty ones?" He looked
at me with disgust and I said, "All right. It looks
to me as if Doewanit was mauled to death by
some big animal. When the androids came here
the first time to abduct the inmates of this
house they had android saber-toothed tigers
with them. My guess is that android saber-
toothed tigers did this." I wasn't telling him
anything he couldn't figure out for himself, but
it sounded good.

He put down the notebook and set the pencil
across it diagonally, as carefully as a French
chef organizing a plate of greens. He said,
"Anybody could go to Superhero Androids and
order up a mess of saber-toothed tigers."

"Anybody who could fill their marble swim-
ming pool with champagne."

"Anybody with money, sure. That's still a lot
of people." He watched me, waiting for me to
wiggle my ears.

I didn't have ears, so I said, "Iron Will might
have something to do with it."

He looked surprised. "You mean the Will Industries guy? Why?"

I told Sergeant Preston the whole situation
surrounding Whipper going back to work for
his father. The police could shake Mr. Will's

cage all they wanted to, and I couldn't lose anything. Somebody, probably Mr. Will, was already trying to kill me. He already wouldn't admit anything. I didn't have anything on him the way I had it on Darken Stormy. Let the police save Zamp and the others if they could. I wasn't proud.

Sergeant Preston said, "Circumstantial evidence won't buy you much. Especially when you have it on a guy with as much pull as Iron Will."

"That's what I thought. That's what he's counting on."

"I could talk to him."

"Don't forget to wear your kid gloves and your velvet pumps."

Angrily, he shoved his notebook and pencil into a pocket and stood up. He said, "And people think people join the cops just to push people around."

"You forgot to say 'nuts.' "

"It's a cliché," he said without smiling. He looked into the kitchen, where one of his men was tickling the telephone with a brush to wash a mouse's teeth with. He said, "I was at home when headquarters called. About to climb into bed with the wife. They said you asked for me special."

"I thought you'd appreciate it."

"Appreciation is not the word."

We watched his men work. One of them came into the living room and pleaded with me to make Bill leave him alone. When Sergeant Preston was about to leave, I stuck out my hand and said, "Still friends?"

"Sure," he said. "What's a little patter under the bridge?"

"Let me know if you squeeze any juice out of Iron Will."

He looked as if I'd put itching powder down his back, but he said he would, and he left in a screaming police car driven by one of his uniformed men.

I stood with my nose about an inch from the closed front door, massaging my wrist. Even at this hour traffic passed on PCH. Two women walked by laughing. In the closet to my left an android of Grampa Zamp was going stale. Behind me was a house as big and empty as the space between stars.

20

Not Murder, Incorporated

I awoke the next morning vigorously scratching my arm and took only a moment to remember where the lip marks had come from. A good night's sleep had not improved my opinion of androids grown from the cells of my grandfather.

I would have liked to discuss the case with Whipper or with Irv Doewanit, but Whipper was too much a part of the action for me to trust his conclusions and old Irv was no longer available for comment. Not even his agent could reach him.

Nothing in the house was worth eating, so I walked down to a coffee shop and had an order of grease. While I chewed on it and tried to force it down with coffee I looked at the pieces in my mental shoe box again. I had a pretty clear picture of what Mr. Will was planning for the people on his elegant and exclusive list, but enough pieces were left over for a whole other puzzle.

I needed to know where the lab was and what would happen there. It was silly of me to hope that I would find Zamp and the surfers there, silly to hope I might even get a chance to throw some grit into Mr. Will's well-oiled machine, but I had a lot of silly hopes, especially when they were all I had.

I sorted through the pieces again. Everybody thought I had enough on them. Mr. Toodemax was so sure that he'd sent his four goons after me. Mr. Will was so sure that he'd sent an android Zamp. Mr. Toodemax was probably taking orders from Mr. Will, but again, Mr. Toodemax might have just gotten cute all on his own.

Why wasn't I as smart as everybody thought I was?

I paid my check, went back to the house to get Bill, and drove a little recklessly along the freeway to Willville.

Traffic was not as thick as the smog on Independence Day, but lumpier. Even following Bill's suggested shortcuts it took me most of the morning to get to Willville. Nothing had changed about it or about the circus around it except that the tacky gaiety was now one day older and one day more forced. The kid who took my money at the parking lot entrance was so perfect he might have been made of wax except that he looked so healthy.

At the main gate I explained that I wasn't here for the entertainment but to see Fran Ignatio at corporate headquarters. The fresh-faced kid found her name on a list, told me where she was, and gave me a ticket that wasn't good for any of the rides, but only for getting into the park. He wished me a nice day.

Bill and I passed the Castle of Android Progress and walked up the Robin Hood street. Bill kept trying to go see something, but I wouldn't let him. We went around the maze, then through the iron gates into Victorian London. Sherlock Holmes was still running around with his magnifying glass, evidently not doing any better with his case than I was doing with mine.

The same android receptionist sat at the desk on the main floor of the Houses of Parliament. The montage of the things Will Industries owned still allowed them to brag about how much money they had without actually showing anybody a balance sheet. I told the receptionist I wanted to see Fran Ignatio and she smiled me through a pair of glass doors. Phoning ahead wasn't necessary. Not to see good ol' Fran.

On the other side of the glass doors was a modern office where another receptionist asked me to wait, Ms. Ignatio would be out in a moment. I stood in front of the reception desk, making us both nervous. I didn't want to sit down. I didn't want to get that comfortable.

A woman almost as wide as she was tall came toward me, rocking as if she were walking the deck of a boat in high seas. She was dressed neatly in black and smelled like soap. A wide green scarf was tied around her neck, one corner dripping fringe from her enormous bosom like a waterfall. Her short white hair was cut in bangs over a pair of wide, intelligent eyes. She would never be beautiful, but that didn't bother her anymore. She was smart and that had gotten her where she was. You probably couldn't get that much information out of a face.

She shook hands with me and told me who she was. I told her who I was. She asked me my business. Right out there in the lobby in front of everybody. You didn't take just any visitor back to the office.

Like some extra in a gangster picture I said, "Irv Doewanit sent me."

She nodded and said, "Why did Mr. Doewanit not come himself?"

"He's a little bit dead."

Nothing in Ms. Ignatio's face changed, but the head of the receptionist snapped around as if yanked by a cord. Fran Ignatio nodded again and said, "If you'll just step back to my office . . . ?" Her incomplete question hung in the air like a spider at the end of a silk filament.

I followed her bulk along a hallway that was painted gray with just enough green in it to give it life and carpeted with the same distinctive color. Paintings of the attractions outside hung on the wall space between doors.

Fran Ignatio's office was nice, but compared to Mr. Will's office this one was a broom closet. It was too small for basketball and the ceiling was not high enough for sky diving. Along one wall windows looked out through slits in the stone facade and let in the kind of bright sunlight they use at amusement parks. Ms. Ignatio settled behind a well-organized desk that had plenty of work on it. Behind her was a low wooden slab supporting three pots of ivy. Above that, on the wall, was a framed poster advertising Superhero Androids. I sat in a customer's chair with padded arms. Bill stood next to me.

Fran Ignatio studied me for what seemed a long time. Typing happened in the next room. At last she said, "Can we have that again about Mr. Doewanit? I'm a little deaf in this ear." She did not indicate which ear.

I said, "Mr. Doewanit was a friend of mine. For one thing, we were in the same business. He was staying at my house out in Malibu. When I came back from an errand I found him on my living room floor. He wasn't doing yoga."

"I'm sorry to hear about that. I did not know Mr. Doewanit well, but our dealings had always been pleasant."

It was my turn to study her. "Is that all?" I said.

"What more should there be? I don't know what you want me to say." Her politely indifferent attitude was setting nicely, like good cement.

"Mr. Doewanit wasn't just staying at my house. He was hiding out. He told me he was hiding out from you."

She almost laughed as she shook her head. "I run the acquisitions department of SA, Mr. Marlowe. That means I look for people who have an appearance and talent that SA may want to promote. Mr. Doewanit had such a talent. We wanted him for our *Great Detectives* series."

"He thought you wanted him a little hard."

"It's true that we pursued him energetically. But we did not kill him. This is Superhero Androids, Mr. Marlowe, not Murder, Incorporated."

I could feel the ground giving way beneath me, but I plunged ahead. I could be just as energetic as she could. I said, "He was killed by an android saber-toothed tiger."

"That changes nothing. Anybody can purchase an android. We do a lot of custom work."

Anybody can buy an android. Sergeant Preston had said the same thing. It was probably even true.

While I was still thinking that, Ms. Ignatio said, "I like your style, Mr. Marlowe."

"Style?" I said. I hoped I didn't look as confused as I felt.

"You and Mr. Doewanit were in the same business. We have an opening in our *Great Detectives* series. Perhaps you would like to fill it." She tossed a thin but very slick catalog at me. I caught it with my lap.

The catalog contained all the detectives I'd ever heard of and many that I hadn't. They dressed in everything from shorts to tuxedos, with a lot of trench coats and brown suits in-between. A few were elflike women with inquisitive eyes.

"I guess I should be honored," I said as I

stood and dropped the catalog on Ms. Ignatio's desk. "But I'm sort of the shy type." I was the type that got the creeps from even thinking about having my cells grown into an android.

She picked up the catalog and slid it into a drawer. "Are you certain? We could make it worth your while."

"If I wanted my while made to be worth something, I would be in a different business."

"The talent for that kind of patter would do it."

"No thanks."

"We'll keep in touch just the same."

"Like you did with Irv Doewanit?"

She didn't like that. She stood up. The interview was over. Bill and I walked to the door, but before we went out I turned with my hand on the knob and said, "I'd like to see Darken Stormy before I go, if I might." I didn't know she was there. I didn't even know she worked in that building. But this time I was lucky.

Fran Ignatio said, "She's busy at the moment, Mr. Marlowe. Please call again." The smile she handed me was calm and professional and meant to hide whatever she was thinking.

I walked along that gray-green corridor trying not to let my head swell too much. Fran Ignatio had told me everything I wanted to know: Darken Stormy worked there and she was at work at the moment. I'm afraid I chuckled a little. Bill chuckled too, though he couldn't know why.

I nodded at both receptionists and out in Victorian London found a phone booth that looked like a small greenhouse, the kind of place where General Sternwood might grow his orchids in *Farewell, My Lovely*. I didn't know that I'd ever seen an orchid. I assumed it was a flower.

Bill reminded me of Darken Stormy's number and I called it. "Darken's not able to come to the phone right now, but if you'll leave your name, your number, and the time you called—" I hung up. I didn't want to leave a message. I had other plans for Darken Stormy's apartment.

21
Mondo Condo

Darken Stormy lived about ten minutes away from Willville in a complex of condominiums that took up three blocks on one side of a wide main street outside the carnival zone. It looked like a small, compact town that could have existed anywhere. A high cinder-block wall kept out the noise and those who made it.

I left the car where I could—wishing again that Bill had a talent for finding parking places—and we walked half a block to a driveway made of identical round gray stones no larger than baseballs. There were two gates, one for in and one for out. To get in, you had to know what code to play on the key pad; to get out, all you had to do was drive up to the gate. It seemed to me that after a car went through the gate took a long time to slide closed. No guard was on duty; there was not even a little house for one. The people who built those condos had too much confidence in their system, and in the stupidity of somebody who might want to buck it. A kid on crutches could get in if he hustled.

I peered at the directory until somebody

drove up, played a sonata on the keypad, and went in past the swinging gate. The car turned a corner and Bill and I strolled in after it. We were three condos away before the gate slammed closed.

Every condo looked the same from the outside—like a big old wood-frame house. They were white and had tasteful gray window frames and doors with a little scrollwork around them. Box hedges grew under each window. All very tidy. All very boring. I followed the numbers down the street and found Darken's condo. Just for the sake of anybody who might be watching, I walked up to the front door and knocked. Nobody home, of course.

In a low voice, I said, "You have a skeleton key for this place, Bill?"

"Me, Boss?" Bill said, sounding shocked. "That would be illegal." A small door in his belly opened, letting loose a cable that whipped around. At the end of the cable was a flat piece of metal with bumps and slots in it.

"Standard equipment?" I said, a little shocked myself.

"It's a diagnostic sensor. Perfectly legal."

"Sure," I said. "It's all in how you use it."

"Right, Boss."

"Open the door, Bill."

"Right, Boss. Watch my dust."

He plugged himself into the door and stood still. I blocked him with my body. Not even the cable moved. Tiny electronic tones came from the keyhole. They stopped and the door clicked.

Bill extracted his diagnostic sensor and it was sucked back into where it had come from. I imagined the eyes of the world were on me. I wanted to look around, but I didn't dare. I had already been standing at the door for a long time. I turned the doorknob and pushed the door with my shoulder. It allowed itself to be pushed and I went inside.

I was in a small entryway blinking into the dimness and the smell. The smell reminded me of the thick human musk at Whipper's house; Darken's place was not a lot cleaner.

Before me, stairs went up to a second floor, each step displaying a shoe or article of clothing. To one side was a dining room with papers and dirty dishes on the table and beyond that a small living room. The kitchen was off the dining room. It had been well used.

A lot of paintings were on the walls, big blotches of color that some people would call art. The furniture was nice, but she'd had it awhile. For reasons of her own Darken had tried to keep the living room more or less clean, though I did find dust. Three books were piled cunningly on an end table, looking more like an exhibit than something she would read. Next to them was a standing photograph of some young guy who had dark curly hair and enough chin to break up ice floes. Scrawled across his hairy arm were the words "To Darken. Always, Danny."

The mantel over the stone fireplace held hundreds of tiny models of automobiles that I had trouble getting Bill not to play with. Still, he followed me around going, "Vroom! Vroom!" softly to himself.

On the wall opposite the fireplace were a lot of photographs in matching frames. Darken, looking pampered and all grown up, was the central figure in each of them. In some she was lounging on shiny new cars, and in others, standing next to people I recognized from TV and movies. In some of them she was being menaced in a theatrical, posed kind of way. One or two even showed her hanging off the arm of Danny, the decorative dude in the photo next to the books.

Upstairs was a bathroom that looked and smelled like the stockroom of a cosmetics concern, and two bedrooms, one of which Darken evidently used for an office. Along with more little autos, photos of Danny the dude were everywhere—in evening clothes, in bathing suits, in some kind of uniform out of a science fiction epic. Unless Darken kept his photo around just to fill space, Bingo had nothing to worry about.

In which case Darken's interest in Whipper must be entirely business. Another piece for the shoe box.

I sat on the top step next to Bill, thinking about those pieces. Nothing new came to me, so I stood up and went through the condo again, this time with a sieve. I opened every door that I could find. I looked in drawers and behind furniture. Behind the desk in the office I found an old dusty phone bill a few months out of date and left it there. I looked into kitchen cupboards. I fought my way through rack after rack of clothing. A couple of cockroaches might have escaped my gaze, but they would have had to be very fast.

When I was done I sat on the top step to wring out my brains again. If Darken Stormy had the "Surf City" music box, she wasn't keeping it here. I tried to make it work that somebody else had taken the music box and killed Irv Doewanit, but I couldn't. She might have mentioned to somebody how much the music box meant to her. She might have mentioned that Whipper Will had it at his house. She might have taken it to the Moon on gossamer wings. Coincidences happened, but for somebody else to want the music box or to know of its importance to Darken and to know where it was located was too much of a coincidence for me. She was as mixed up with this as chocolate chips were in a chocolate-chip cookie.

I walked slowly down the stairs, one heavy step at a time. Of course, I didn't *have* to find what I was looking for. It wasn't a *rule* that the big shot detective had to succeed.

I was about halfway to the bottom of both the stairs and my mood when a key rattled in the front-door lock and knocked the blues out of me. I froze and did my best to think like Philip Marlowe. He might have said some magical detective thing and disappeared in a puff of classic black-and-white smoke, but all I could do was stand there and let her pin me with her eyes. It was Darken Stormy, dressed in a very businesslike gray suit and carrying a black briefcase.

The expression of astonishment and concern on her face made her look like a little girl, despite all the paint. When she recognized me the astonishment and concern drained away, leaving only anger. Anger did not suit her.

She did not say anything to me but crossed to the wide window between the kitchen and the dining room, and picked up the white phone that sat on the counter. When she lifted the phone from the cradle, I said, "You may not want to call the police after you hear what I have to say."

Indecision worked so strongly in her that she almost vibrated. She wanted to chew her lip, but she didn't want to muss her lipstick, so she just twitched it. She put the phone down and tried to drill me with her eyes, but not even she was that good. "All right," she said, and crossed her arms.

"Irv Doewanit is dead."

Her mouth had stopped twitching. She said, "Who?"

I shook my head. There was no reason she should have known Irv. I started again. "Somebody stole the music box."

"What music box?"

I smiled and said, "Very good. You really are an actress, aren't you? Very good, but not very smart."

"Maybe the police can figure out what you're

talking about," she said, and lay her hand on the telephone. It lay there for a while and didn't pick up the receiver.

I said, "You seem to have caught me at a little burglary, Ms. Stormy, but I still think we can do business. After all, Irv Doewanit is dead and you made it happen."

Red fingernails swiftly tapped on the telephone. Darken Stormy said, "I still don't know who Irv Doewanit is." She was getting control of herself again. She was playing the moment as if it were a scene out of *Charlie Sundown*. "But I do know that you are a boring little man. Or maybe you're just boring." She couldn't help smiling. I was gratified that Bill didn't laugh.

"Irv Doewanit is the guy who was at my house when whoever you sent to get the 'Surf City' music box tried to pick it up. Irv must have objected. I found a piece of the music box in his fist."

"Make me care."

"I don't know anybody else who would kill for that music box. Do you?"

"I wouldn't kill for it. I'm not a killer."

"No," I said, "but you're the perfect suspect."

Her breath came in sharply and then she closed her mouth over it. She unfolded her arms and pulled her briefcase up onto the dining room table. She opened it and stood with her back to me while she looked inside as if a crystal ball were in there. "And you want to help me, right? What's in it for you besides I don't report you to the police for breaking and entering?"

"Where are the surfers and my grampa Zamp?"

She pushed around some papers on the dining-room table, selected a few, and put them into her briefcase. Without turning around, she said, "Maybe I don't know."

"Maybe. The police might see it differently."

"Blackmail."

"A funny kind of blackmail. I just want to do good."

She snapped her briefcase shut and turned to look at me with it dangling from both hands in front of her. "Look," she said, "Mr. Marlowe. I don't know where they are. If you want to talk to the police, please be my guest. We wouldn't be having this conversation if you'd found the music box here. You wouldn't find it here because it's not here. That makes it considerably more difficult for you to connect me with the murder of your friend. Maybe impossible. I have alibis. I have friends. And most importantly of all, I didn't do it."

She strutted to the door like Miss America on the runway, and looked at me over her shoulder. "Coming?" she said. She opened the door and held it wide as Bill and I slid out past her. After pulling the door closed with a bang she came down the walk and stood with us next to her car. It was low and red and had enough sex appeal to get whistles at a stag party.

Darken said, "So, how did you get in, any-way?"

I shook my head and smiled.

She shrugged and said, "OK. Just don't pass the information around. This place isn't much, but it's home."

"As long as you pay your own rent."

She patted me lightly on one cheek and showed me plenty of black-stockinged leg as she got into her car. The engine caught on the first try and a window hummed as it went down. She said, "Mr. Will isn't a killer either."

"That's what Whipper keeps telling me."

She gave me one of her atomic smiles as the window hummed up. The car rolled slowly away from the curb, then suddenly took off as if somebody had thrown a rock at it. It screeched around the corner and soon even the sound of its engine was gone.

"Gosh," said Bill. "What a babe."

There was nothing so very special about the way Darken Stormy drove her car down the street. Except that as she pulled away I got the clue I'd been waiting for.

22

Clue in a Bun

On the rear bumper of Darken Stormy's slinky little car was a sticker like the one on the back of ID Advertising truck number eighty-two. It said STOP TRUCK STOP. I still didn't know what that meant, but it must mean something. I wasn't buying any new coincidences today.

I said, "Anything in your bubble memory about Stop Truck Stop?"

"It's a truck stop," Bill said.

"I get it," I said. "You're Abbott and I'm Costello. Now I'm supposed to say, 'What's a truck stop?' and you say, 'brakes,' and I get very excited and the audience goes crazy with laughter."

"If you say so, Boss."

This seemed the day for me to start all wrong. I said, "OK, Bill. Forget all that. Tell me about Stop Truck Stop."

"It's a truck stop," Bill said.

He seemed serious, but I still felt as if I'd fallen into the middle of "Who's on First?" Hoping for the best, I said, "What's a truck stop?"

"It's a place where long-haul truck drivers stop to eat and get gas." He laughed.

I interrupted when I said, "You know where the Stop Truck Stop is?"

"Sure, Boss. It's in L.A. County."

That meant it was in his bubble memory. "Let's go there right now."

Without Bill's help I found my way back onto the Santa Ana Freeway and rode it north past square glass buildings that looked very proud to be so clean, and shopping malls that were no more than pimples in the middle of oceans of flash. Evidently Melt-O-Mobiles did not sell as well out here as they did in the more fashionable parts of town.

The buildings got bigger and dirtier, and soon we were creeping through downtown with sunlight reflecting into my eyes from tall buildings that were half-empty because nobody needed all those tall buildings except the construction companies that built them. Cars changed lanes seemingly at random and without bothering to signal. As I jockeyed into the proper lane for the Hollywood Freeway, some genius rushed up in a big cream Continental to sit on my bumper and honk in a way that made me slow down. The Continental swung angrily into the lane next to mine, cutting off somebody who also owned a horn, made a nasty remark to me with one finger, and got off at Fifth Street.

We rode through canyons of ivy that had the dusty remains of old Hollywood hovering above them. After the Hollywood Bowl turnoff, we were in the valley and the traffic thinned a little. That was OK because the air got hotter, making driving just as unpleasant.

We rode through a lot of light industry and tract houses, and then the hills closed in around us like the contours of reclining green women. Up near Sylmar, Bill told me to turn off. The offramp let me out onto a hot wide street that carried as many trucks as cars. The trucks thundered by like eldritch gods, making the wind to blow and the ground to shake.

I passed sheds that were too big to enjoy the luxury of looking like sheds and yards full of diseased-looking automobile hulks. This stuff went on mile after mile, like a blighted forest.

I saw the sign before Bill told me where to turn. It was three or four stories tall—tall enough to be seen from the freeway if anybody were looking for it—and set on a tripod that made it look like a war machine from a science fiction movie. In neon that looked faded in the sunlight the sign said STOP TRUCK STOP, and in smaller letters, WELCOME, PARDNER!

I turned into the large parking lot, most of which was taken up with trucks, some of which were long enough to extend into the next county. In one corner of the lot was a square one-story building with brown shingles over the windows like bangs. Through the big windows I could see people eating. The smell of cooking grease boiled out of rotating turban vents on the roof like some genie hired to bring in the customers. I remembered how hungry I was.

Next to the restaurant was a gas station, inside which everything was a little too big to be real. It was designed for the use of giants.

I had driven a long way to get here, but I felt no closer to the lab or to the people I was looking for than I had at Darken Stormy's apartment.

I parked the Belvedere and just sat listening to the engine be off for a change. Warm wind carried the smell of burgers and fries through the car. Now that we were stopped, Bill hung out the window like a dog. I wanted to think, but my brain was too tired and crowded with maybes.

It had taken me a lot of work to get this far. Not only had I not saved anybody, but Irv Doewanit was dead and Zamp had been taken away too. Mr. Will could do a lot of terrible things to Zamp and the rest. If the courts got hold of this case, they would have fun deciding what Zamp was and whether laws about humans applied. I rolled up the windows, cracked the door of the Belvedere, and got out.

The heat of the asphalt came up through my shoes as Bill and I walked across to the restaurant. Behind me and to one side a truck coughed, rumbled, and then settled into an idle I could have danced to had I been in the mood.

The restaurant was cold and thick with the greasy smell of short-order cooking. The gabble of talking was almost as thick—it was a busy place. Occasionally one of the cooks would shout a number and a waitress would wander back to pick up plates that she would arrange up and down her arms and take out to a table. A few families sat in booths. They were sunburned and tired-looking and either eager to get back on the road or stretching that last cup of coffee to avoid it.

Most of the customers were truckers and they liked to eat at the long counter that curved along two sides of the room. They came in all shapes and sizes, but they were generally big men who wore workshirts or plaids loud enough to keep them awake on long, lonely drives. Hats were popular and seemed to be about equally split between the baseball and the cowboy variety. If there was a no-smoking section, I never found it.

A thin woman wearing a uniform in two shades of coffee walked up to me. Her shoes were ugly enough to be comfortable and she wore a lace fan on her chest that was big enough to cool the king of Siam. Her wrinkled horsey face was all business. "Table for two?" she said, looking at a spot between me and Bill.

"Not just yet," I said. "I'd like to talk to the manager."

She glanced behind me and said, "One?"

"Counter's OK, Mabel," said a big guy in a voice like a squeaky wheel. He nodded to us as he lumbered by.

"I'm the manager," she said. She wasn't chewing gum, but I'd have sworn she snapped it then. "What's the problem?"

"I'm a detective working on a case—"

"That's nice, honey. Three?" She was looking over my shoulder again.

She showed a man, a woman, and a very skinny kid to a table, and came back. Evidently I was not the most important person in her life. We were interrupted five more times before I found out that she knew nothing about Superhero Androids or any lab.

"I seen them androids on the news." She shook her head as if over somebody who wore diesel-powered underwear. "There's a lab down at the college in Pasadena," she said, really trying to help. "Two?" she asked the space behind me.

When she came back I told her we'd like to sit at the counter. She nodded and stepped aside. We were no longer of any interest to her whatsoever.

Bill and I sat at the counter. I ordered a Stop Burger for me—advertised as the best burger in the galaxy—and an order of fries for Bill, which I would eat. The guy next to me was about the same age as Whipper Will, but had more muscles. I said, "Howdy."

"Howdy," he said, swallowing the word as if he regretted having said it.

"You know this territory?" I said.

"Some."

"Know anything about a lab?"

"You mean a Labrador retreiver? I got a shepherd, myself. But he's at home keeping the wife honest." He chuckled as he sipped his coffee, then puffed a cigarette that had been burning in a glass tray. The smell was manly, but I'd rather have had Brillo stuffed up my nose.

I talked to the fellow on Bill's other side, but got an answer that was just as meaningful.

The burger came, and it was a thick, juicy job. The waitress took the time to watch me bite into it. I nodded as I chewed, and as soon as I could grab a mouthful of air, I said, "You're right. It is the best burger in the galaxy."

She watched me just a shade too long and said, "I guess you would know, at that." Looking thoughtful, she marched off to fill coffee cups.

Bill swished fries in catsup and gave them to me one at a time. They were good too. While I ate I looked around, just enjoying the atmosphere. What I saw out the window made me stop chewing.

On the side of the restaurant away from the parking lot and the gas station was another wrecking yard like many others I'd seen that day, but full of display signs instead of automobiles. From where I sat I couldn't see much but a row of big white buckets-o'-chicken, like a row of grounded water towers.

Without hurry I finished the burger and fries, paid my check, and walked out of the restaurant. As I touched the door Mabel suggested I have a nice day. My chances of following her advice had just improved. Bill and I walked around the restaurant on the street side and went just far enough so that I could see the big sign yard.

Doughnuts like airplane wheels sat on the ground near a bunch of monster spear points that I finally figured out were ice-cream cones. Lined up in rows like slices of toast were neon signs, square blocks of plastic, painted wooden planks, signs advertising grocery stores and gas stations. They were too big to be sitting on the ground. Like the gas station designed for use by trucks, the sign yard did not look quite real.

A sign that looked more normal because it was raised on a big metal stand stood at the gate. It said SIGN OF THE TIMES SIGN CEMETERY. To Bill I said, "Recognize it?"

"Sure, Boss."

Sure. We had seen a photograph of it at Willville on the wall-sized montage of all the pretty things Will Industries owned. And just to ease away any doubts that this was the place I was looking for, an ID Advertising truck was parked in the Sign of the Times lot. A bumper sticker was on the back bumper. I couldn't read it from where I stood, but I was willing to bet it said STOP TRUCK STOP. Mabel or her employees had been busy.

In my brain I spread out a map of Los Angeles County, sat down with myself, and began to figure. I'd waited about an hour for ID Advertising truck number eighty-two to return to the storage yard in Pasadena. I thought it had gone to Willville from the Convention Center and then to the yard. The truck would have taken about the same amount of time to go from the Con-

vention Center to the Sign of the Times Sign
Cemetery and then home.

I was starting to believe that Zamp and the
surfers were around here someplace. In the lab.
I shuddered and thought about all the hours till
ten-thirty the next morning.

Across the street from the sign yard were six
shabby buildings the color of a sick person's
tongue, seemingly huddled together for comfort. The ensemble was called the Shady Pines
Motel, but the only pine around was a single
specimen in front of the office. It was made
from cement and was faded and not very convincing. It had probably not been very convincing when new. Hanging below the motel sign
was another that said VACANCY.

I drove the Belvedere into the lot of the Shady
Pines Motel and entered the office. I talked to a
large woman who had no chin but a cloud of
hair that was so blond it was almost yellow. It
looked as natural as the pine tree out front. She
took enough money for two nights and gave me
a key. It didn't bother her that I had no luggage,
and she didn't charge me for Bill. I moved the
car back to the space in front of number twenty-
eight.

The room was clean and plain and had all the
personality of a plastic spoon. While Bill made
patterns on the sink with the tiny bars of soap
he'd found, I sat on the edge of the bed feeling
the rough nap of the coverlet with my fingers
and thinking about the lab and the list on Mr.
Will's desk. I thought about Zamp and the surf-

ers and all the unpleasant experiments that
could be done on them. I thought of Irv Doewanit dead on the living-room floor and the
things people will do for sentiment. Max Toodemax grinned at me evilly from the window of
an empty beach house.

I decided that what I was doing made as much
sense as what Bill was doing. I sat by the window and watched the Sign of the Times Sign
Cemetery. After a while the ID Advertising
truck left. The sun went down and when the
yard was just a gray uncertainty, it was suddenly filled with hard white light that splashed
from tall metal poles. In the spaces between
traffic I could hear the lamps buzzing.

I sat in my dark room and started to imagine
large, many-armed insects crawling out from
behind the disused signs across the street.
When one of them waved at me, I went to bed.

23

Burning Daylight

I slept without dreaming and the next morning felt as if I'd gotten the good night's sleep I'd paid for. I washed and dressed and took Bill across the street to the Stop Truck Stop, where I ordered the Trucker's Breakfast, a not very subtle combination of eggs, meat, pancakes, and coffee. It was a lot of food, but I ate it all. I didn't know when I would eat again.

It was a quarter to ten. Something would begin at the lab in forty-five minutes. Despite the figuring I'd done with my mental map the previous afternoon it suddenly seemed like a real long shot that the event would happen anywhere near here. The time element may have had nothing to do with where the truck had been. This hot stretch of truck-distressed road was not a neighborhood for laboratories, except the kind that screams came from in the middle of the night. I thought that and immediately wished I hadn't.

All I had was the long shot. I could take it or go back to Malibu and sit by the phone. I took it.

"Come on, Bill," I said. "We're burning daylight."

We walked in at the open gate of the Sign of the Times Sign Cemetery and drifted across the lot. Parked in it now were Darken Stormy's red sports car and three long black limousines, as cold and businesslike as loaded pistols. I whistled at them. Sometimes the long shots pay off. I figured I was past due.

In the center of the lot was an office, a wooden box made of mismatched boards that had not been painted lately. I went in and let the door slap shut behind me. At the back of the office was another closed door. Over it on a shelf was a TV, turned low but showing a quiz show.

On one wall was a small desk under a calendar featuring an improbable young woman wearing a smile and a pair of very clean bib overalls that were very short at the bottom and fell open at the top. She was holding a wrench and leaning over a car engine as if to fix it. She'd have lots of help.

On the desk were two wire baskets, both filled with stiff yellowing papers. One stack was weighted by a big metal gear. The blotter was marked with cigarette burns and gouges.

Along the other wall, under a window so dirty it hardly deserved the name, was a long wooden workbench. Tools hung from a rack and others were strewn out along the bench. In the center of some open work space, along with a plastic bottle of glue and a few squares of sandpaper, was the "Surf City" music box, the tip of the blue wooden wave missing.

Watching me from a wooden chair that had only one arm was Danny, Darken Stormy's boyfriend. His coverall had grease down its front as if that was where he wiped his hands. On his chest was a plastic bar that said DANNY MACABRE.

I listened to the TV murmuring for a moment and then a little contemptuously said, "This doesn't look like the kind of business Will Industries would get involved in." I didn't drag a white glove across his desk, but hoped my tone suggested it was only a matter of time.

Instead of answering me Danny stood up and said, "Can I help you?" as if helping me was not his fondest wish. He was a big guy, but his voice had no more substance than a Saltine.

I said, "I'm here for the meeting in the lab."

He sat down in the chair and rocked, making bad music with the springs, and picked up a clipboard from his desk. "Name?" he said.

"Em Shannon." Mr. Shannon ran a computer software company. His name had been on the list.

Danny threw down the clipboard and said, "I don't know what your game is, mister, but you aren't Em Shannon or anybody else on this list. They're all already down at the meeting." He laughed. "Besides, you're not dressed for the gig. Besides, Mr. Will doesn't like bots."

"What does Darken Stormy think of them?"

"Who's Darken Stormy?" he said without interest. But he was rocking fast now.

"You should have said, 'What's a Darken Stormy?' It would have been more convincing."

He puckered his lips and glanced at the workbench. If I hadn't known how important the music box was, the gesture would have seemed meaningless. He said, "She isn't here."

"Then somebody else must be driving her car."

Danny decided something and then said slowly, "Is there a joke here someplace?"

"If there is, it's on you and Darken." I glanced at my watch. It was almost ten. I needed answers fast. Danny frowned and I demanded, "Where's that meeting?"

"What meeting?"

"The meeting that everybody is already at."

"Nix," he said, and shook his head.

"Oh, gangster stuff, huh? Has Darken told you how involved she is with the scragging of Irv Doewanit?"

His eyes got big and wild. He leaned forward and his feet dropped flat on the floor. "No," he said, barely making sound.

"I found him dead on my living-room floor. He had the missing piece of that music box in his hand."

"So?"

I shook my head. "Not smart, Danny. Nobody in the world but Darken would want that music box bad enough to kill for it. She knows that. We've already discussed it. She thought she was safe because I wasn't able to find the music box at her condo."

He glanced at the music box again. This time he knew I knew what the glance meant. He said, "Why should I care about her?"

"Not smart again. Pictures of you and her together are all over her house. There's the music box. A case can be made that you're pretty chummy."

"Things disappear."

Bluffing, I said, "I don't really need the box itself. I have witnesses who saw Darken ask for the box and other witnesses who know what it means to her." I didn't tell him that my witnesses were what I was looking for, and that if he smartened up I would have nothing better to do than go home and clip coupons.

"All right," he said.

"Don't look so glum. Darken doesn't have to swing for the murder. It's possible she didn't even order Doewanit killed, but the person she sent for the music box got a little overenthusiastic. You'll need help proving it, though. Personally, I can go either way." I snapped my fingers and said, "You didn't ice Irv, did you?"

He looked so genuinely shocked that I thought his surprise must be real. He said, "How much?"

"Is money all you can think about? Where is that meeting being held?"

He watched a fly buzz on the dirty window, while sitting so still the chair didn't make a noise. He looked at me and put his tongue out to one side between his teeth. He made as nice a variety of thoughtful gestures as I'd ever seen. Probably he'd learned them in acting school.

After running through the repertoire twice he stood up, but despite his bulk was no more threatening than a Saint Bernard. From a corner he grabbed a flashlight the size of a celery stalk and said, "Come on." He pushed past me and Bill out the door.

Outside, heat was gathering like evil spirits. We made a parade through it past the limousines and the red sports car and into the aisles of old signs. Danny threaded us among an alphabet of letters in different styles and colors. Just sitting there on the ground, they towered above us as if we were ants on a model train layout. He took us down a row of big orange balls, yellow seashells, and red horses with wings. At the end were a few rectangular plastic slabs; through the cracked-out places I could see fluorescent tubes.

Near the back fence, signs lay in dusty stacks, forgotten as the businesses they once fronted. Danny Macabre found what he was looking for between one of the stacks and a big neon hamburger with most of its tubes gone. Lying flat on the ground was a weathered wooden sign, no more than a collection of splinters waiting for a careless finger. The ghost of paint that remained on it said BONANZA FEED AND GRAIN.

He looked around, but there was nothing to see except old signs. We were protected on all sides. As if from far away came the sound of trucks rolling by on the street. The smell from the truck stop was a heavy blanket that closed in on us as surely as did the old signs.

"I'll get in trouble," Danny Macabre said, his voice no thicker than a piece of paper.

"You're in trouble now," I said, and tried to make it stick. "But your trouble is a stroll in the park compared to the fix Darken Stormy is in."

Danny handed me the flashlight, then leaned down and grabbed a metal handle that was much newer than the sign. He used body English to heave the sign upward. It opened easily like the door on the storm shelter in *The Wizard of Oz* and stuck out like a wing. Below it was a flight of cement stairs that led into the ground.

"I'll be lucky if Mr. Will just fires me." He was breathing hard.

In all that heat something blew across my back and made me shiver. Trying to sound gruff, I said, "You'll never know till you try. Let's get to it."

24

Come as You Are

Danny Macabre took back the flashlight and led the way down the steps. Bill went next. I came last so that I could watch everybody. I trusted Bill, but he was easily distracted. I trusted Danny no more than I'd trust any cornered animal.

The steps went down one flight or so and we were at the end of a long, crooked tunnel held in place by square wooden rafters and supports. The beam of the flashlight pointed things out like a bony finger. On the dusty floor a few tracks led off into the dimness then back out again. As far as I could tell all the tracks had been made by the same pair of shoes.

"Not much business," I said. "There must be a VIP entrance somewhere else."

Danny's voice shook a little when he said, "We wouldn't have a chance at the front door. Nobody watches this way." He smiled without heat. "Nobody else knows about it. Not even Mr. Will. Back in the fifties this was some kind of Civil Defense project. I found it while moving stuff around out here one day."

"Civil Defense?" I said.

"You know. The Rooskies were gonna bomb us back to the Stone Age." He watched my face. Like his, I suppose it looked a little gray in the feeble light coming from above. "Or maybe you don't know."

"Don't get too clever with the guessing," I said. "Let's go." After a few steps I told Bill to turn on his eyelights. Between Bill's eyes and Danny Macabre's flash we could see everything there was to see, which wasn't much.

The tunnel went on for a while. The air down here was cool and smelled of damp dead things. In a few places water oozed out of the wall. We came to a dead end against which yellow cans were stacked. Each of them said something like CREAMED CORN or ROAST BEEF HASH on it in red block letters above a triangle containing the letters CD. A few of the cans were open and empty and stacked neatly against a side wall.

Across from the empty cans was a dark doorway crossed by rough boards hung with a sheer curtain of spider silk.

"Careful where you put your hands and feet," Danny said, and climbed carefully around the boards.

Bill climbed through eagerly, and I followed as if the boards were electrified. We stood in another tunnel, this one much narrower and dirtier. In this dank place the artificial light we carried seemed as bright as sunlight. It made shadows that danced and quivered across the walls and floor. Bill looked around, showing us that the walls were widely spaced wooden planks, and that the occasional braces thrust out at odd angles, all but blocking our path. Small things moved in the emptiness beyond the light. If it had been more cramped the tunnel could have been a California basement.

As we moved along slowly I whispered to Bill, "Anything about this place in your bubble memory?"

"Sorry, Boss."

We kept walking. I saw the tails of departing rats—which is the way I like them—and nests of nightmare insects. Far away I heard howling which I liked to think was wind.

When we came to a wall that had slits of light around what was apparently a narrow door, Danny turned off his light and asked Bill to do the same. I repeated Danny's order for Bill's benefit. The darkness leapt in at us. I stood very still, sniffing the wood and the damp and the small nasty creatures, and listening to the howling. I could hear the creak of Danny's shoe leather and the breathing of two people. Then I heard the rumble of conversation and running water. Somebody flushed a toilet just past my left shoulder.

"Look here," Danny said. Danny's pointing hand was silhouetted in a gray oblong framed by the bright slits. As my eyes grew used to the darkness I began to see something on the oblong. I blinked and suddenly what I saw was not on the oblong but on the other side of it. "One-way glass," said Danny, proud as if he'd invented it.

Beyond the glass was a wide green aisle with narrow metal cabinets on each side—lockers, I thought. A couple of large old naked men were drying themselves with towels, each with a foot raised onto a yellow bench that ran down the center of the aisle. More water came on. It sounded like a shower.

"Civil Defense?" I whispered.

"If you have a better idea, mister, I'd like to hear it."

After a while the two naked men got dressed and went away. Other naked men walked by but none of them stopped in our aisle. Danny jiggled a catch and pushed open the glass, which was hung on hinges like a door. We tumbled out quickly and he pushed a mirror closed behind us. The room was warm and humid and smelled like the chlorine Whipper Will used to keep his yoyogurt equipment clean. The green stuff on the floor was artificial grass.

A few aisles away a loud male voice said, "I'm his manager. I'm gonna get him a fight with a guy in a wheelchair and who's blind in one eye." Somebody else laughed and said, "Reuben's bullshit." That drew more laughter. In the shower room somebody began to sing in a goofy voice, "Sing to me! The song I've been waiting to hear!" in a key of his own invention.

I prodded Danny and said, "Are we going to stay for the next show, or do we keep moving?"

"Yeah," he said. He led us to another aisle. A

geek wearing glasses and a single black sock
was sitting on a yellow bench. He looked at us,
got embarrassed, then went back to picking at
the toes of his naked foot.

Danny took us into an aisle where nobody
was changing and fiddled with a combination
lock. "My lock," he said as he pulled open
the door. Inside was a stairway the width of
the locker. Danny went in, then Bill, then me.
I pulled the door closed behind us. Danny hung
his lock from the inside handle and pushed it
closed until it clicked.

The air got cool as we hurried down the
stairs. By the time we got to the bottom we had
the flashlight and the eyelights working again.
We were at the end of a tunnel with finished
stone walls like the ones in the Castle of Android Progress. It angled downward. At the low-
est point was a puddle that we had to leap over.
We angled up for a while and came to an empty
room. One wall was made of dull black metal,
but somebody had taken the trouble to cut a
hole in it with a torch, proving again that human curiosity would bear a lot of weight. Something with no more reality than black smoke
covered the other side of the hole.

Danny Macabre walked to the hole and
pointed to it as if he were a TV weatherman.
He said, "Go in through here. You'll be in a big
stone room. In the middle of the room is a hydraulic lift. Against the wall near the lift is a
narrow ladder. You can take that up to the
meeting."

"What about you?"

"I'll wait here."

"For how long? A minute? Three?"

Danny shook his head and said, "I'm not a bad person."

I took a good look at him. He didn't look like a bad person, but the idea that you could tell the good guys from the bad guys by the heft of their eyebrows was a notion I'd gotten only from television. "Not bad," I said. "But looking out for yourself like anybody else."

"I'll come with you, then."

He'd suggested it too quickly, but I had to admit we didn't have a wide range of choices. It had to be one or the other. He had to come or stay. The mental coin flipped and came down. I took a deep breath and said, "OK. We've come this far."

He grinned for some reason and stepped through the hole. There was light on the other side, then darkness again. I told Bill, "Squawk if anything looks wrong to you."

It was a dangerous order, but Bill said, "Right, Boss," and went through. The light faded in and out again. No squawk. No clang as Bill hit the deck. I swallowed and went through myself.

I had to push aside a curtain heavy as the chairman of the board's carpet and came out in another stone room, this one wide enough to comfortably fit a commercial jet and long enough to make that width look narrow. Light came from behind, coping about halfway up the walls, higher than a gorilla could reach. In the center of the room was the shiny steel pillar of a hydraulic lift. I followed it up with my eyes and lost it in shadow. Around the pillar were lab benches set up for heavy-duty experimentation. Beyond the benches was a vat with a catwalk over it and a big machine leaning over it like a cat over a fishbowl. The smell told me it was a vat of android ur-glop. On the wall next to the hydraulic lift was a metal ladder so narrow and fragile it looked as if a monkey would have trouble climbing it. Across from the ladder was a wall with bars in it—a line of three cells with stout stone walls between them. Sniffling and moaning came from one of the cells. The sounds made my flesh crawl.

I stood motionless next to Danny and Bill, trying not to apply too much meaning to the squeamish sound. Behind us was a midnight blue curtain embroidered with a picture of a pearly white horse that had a horn in the middle of its forehead and a beard like a swirl of whipped cream. It was sitting among stiff artificial trees and small woodland creatures that would look more natural with wind-up keys in their backs.

"The lab," I said in a voice like the stirring of dead leaves.

"Yeah," said Danny. "There's your ladder. I'm not going up it, not for you or for Darken or for anybody."

"You must know what's at the top."

He spoke in the flat tone of a man repeating a bus schedule that he'd memorized, not because he wanted to, but just because he'd said it so often. "I told you," he said. "Mr. Will's conference room. I went up once just out of curiosity, and looked in through an air duct in the wall. It's a long way up and a longer way down." He shuddered. "I don't want to climb it again."

"Hello, out there," came a voice. Danny and I jumped a little, I'm afraid. No one in our party had spoken.

Unless someone was playing hidey-hole under a lab bench the voice had to have come from one of the cells. Danny and Bill stayed by the curtain while I sidled across the room, my hearts banging against each other like castanets. I knew that voice and it meant I had been right about a few things for a change.

Standing in the center of any of the cells, a big man would not quite be able to touch both side walls at once with his fingertips. Worked into the door of each cell was a square panel of black metal the size of a paperback novel. In the center of each panel was a keyhole big enough for my fist.

As I approached the nearest cell a dozen hands reached out of the center one and gripped the bars, followed by the surprised faces of six women. Two of them didn't know whether to be horrified or encouraged. One woman was a blonde and the other was a brunette. The brunette was old and had not brooked much nonsense in her life. The blonde might ordinarily have been pretty, but at the moment her face looked like an empty sandbox. Their hair had not been done that morning. "Who are you?" the brunette called as if she was used to getting answers.

I knew the other four women. They were the surfer girls. Bingo cried, "Zoot!" The other surfer girls did the same. The two strangers looked at them as if somebody had lost her mind.

I tipped my hat at them and looked into the cell on the near end. It was big, but no larger than Mr. Will's private office. Inside the cell were five men, a Toomler, and a camel. I knew from the smell the camel would be there. Zamp and the men were wearing what they'd had on when they were picked up. Max Toodemax wore a short-sleeved knit shirt with a green worm on the pocket. His fawn gray pants had once been cleaner and less wrinkled. The three missing surfers were dressed in the uniform. Captain Hook grumbled something about it being about time. Knighten Daise, very much the camel, still wore his Foreign Legion hat.

I stepped toward the cell, dreamy as a guy in a hair dye commercial. Zamp stood three feet away from me on the other side of the bars. He said, "So?"

I said, "So, nu, already?" I was very glad to see him. He reached for the bars and I put my hands over his. He was shaking. I probably was too.

"I'm all right. Get us out of here."

I didn't move. I just said, "I guess you got to see terrible old Earth after all."

"Yeah." He nodded, giving me my philosophical point.

While he was doing that another man stepped forward. He was wearing a dark suit, but his tie was off and his white shirt was open. It was Iron Will, Whipper Will's father, the man who a lot of people thought was behind this mess. Of course I hadn't thought that for a while.

I could see everybody's neck. I didn't see any blue plastic collars. The case was shaping up nicely.

"Marlowe," Mr. Daise said in his thick flat camel voice.

"Good afternoon, Mr. Daise," I said. I patted Zamp's hands, said, "I'll be right back," and moved down to the third cell. I immediately wished I hadn't. This was where the sniffling and moaning came from, and it smelled as if someone had been sick very thoroughly there, and for a long time.

Quite a crowd was in that cell, but I had difficulty sorting them out. The truth is, I didn't try very hard. One creature had an extra arm growing from a shoulder. Another had two heads, one fairly normal, the other with teeth like tombstones, a nose like a mashed turnip, and wild red eyes. The sniffing came in wet waves from the nose. One of the things in the cell was barely a puddle, an unbaked cookie of a person. The moaning came from a thing like a knot of snakes that struggled against the eight shackles holding it against the wall. Maybe I wasn't enough of a humanitarian. Maybe they should have sent Mr. Keen, Tracer of Lost Persons, or Dr. Christian. I turned away.

Bill and Danny were gawking into the cells. Danny glanced into the third one and came back looking a little green. I let Bill look, but what he saw seemed to have no effect on him. The three of us stood where everybody could see us. Danny kept looking between me and Zamp as if we were a Ping-Pong match. He didn't ask if we were related, but he wanted to.

To Danny, I said, "You should have told me they were here. I would have walked a little faster."

"You didn't say you wanted them. You just talked about Mr. Will's big meeting."

"Who does that fellow in the suit look like to you?"

He took a good look for what must have been the first time, and his face went from green to pasty white. His mouth fell open wide enough to take in a candlestick. Then he swore softly.

"Take it easy, Danny. He'll probably give you your very own android for helping save him."

Mr. Will almost choked on a short, cynical laugh.

Mr. Daise said, "Are you planning to let us out anytime soon?"

Mr. Will said, "A key should be in a niche beyond the third cell."

I went to look for it, being very careful to stare straight ahead and not breathe too deeply till I had gotten past the monsters.

I found the key behind a small wooden box hung on the wall. It was a big cast-iron job that should have been hanging on the wall of the sheriff's office in Dodge City. I went back and let everybody out. They had no luggage. Zamp and I rubbed noses until we both became embarrassed and stopped.

I looked at my watch. Ten-seventeen. I made a vague motion at Bill and Danny and said, "I'm going to send all of you back to my motel with these two gentlemen." I guess I still didn't trust Danny Macabre. "Wait for me there while I take a look upstairs."

"I'll come with you," Zamp said.

"Haven't you had enough?"

"More than enough. It's slopping over the sides and making dirty on the floor. But I want to see this through."

I didn't have time to argue with him. And the energy I had I'd probably need. I said, "No."

"Why?"

"What are you going to do, Zamp? Stow away in my pocket?"

He began to get angry, then changed his mind. He smiled as if bearing up well under pain and walked across the room to ostentatiously study the fancy curtain we'd come through.

"You know what's up there?" Mr. Will said.

I nodded and said, "I'm kind of a detective."

"You must be. You're also an optimist." He smiled. It had warmth and looked as if it belonged on that face, a pleasant change from what I had been getting from somebody who looked like him.

Flopsie (or was it Mopsie?) pointed into the third cell without looking at it and said, "What about them?"

"Mistakes," Mr. Will said, his mouth set into a line.

Mopsie (or was it Flopsie?) had proposed a difficult ethical question. I took the easy way out. I said, "Leave 'em." Nobody argued with me.

I gave Bill the key to my motel room and told him to let everybody in. They could all watch each other. While they congregated by the curtain Danny Macabre came up to shake my hand. While he did it, he whispered, "What about the camel? There's no room for him in the tunnel. How will I explain him if we get caught in the locker room?"

"It's a men's locker room, isn't it? I'd worry more about the women."

He gulped and his eyes got wide. I said, "Go. A lot of clever people will be with you. You'll figure out something."

He let go of my hand and went. I watched them go behind the curtain one by one and be gone as if by magic. Even Mr. Daise made it, though he complained all the while about the tight fit. When I was alone I went to the narrow ladder, the one Danny Macabre said he never wanted to climb again. I had saved Zamp and my friends. Now it was time to see if I was good enough to save Los Angeles. I grabbed a rung and started up.

25
Room at the Top

I climbed in light for a while, working up a sweat. The ladder had been built for Earth people so the rungs were a little too far apart for me to be comfortable using them. But I was a tough guy. I kept climbing. The silver column of the hydraulic lift was with me, looking very much the same at this level as it did below.

Just before I entered the shadow at the top of the room I looked down on the laboratory, on the light tubes behind their coping, on the two empty cells and the one full one, on the vat. I could hear the things in the full cell breathing noisily and moving around. Somebody's failed experiments. Somebody without enough guts to put them out of their misery, but with too much of what some people might think was compassion. It was a judgment call. I didn't have an easy answer myself. I just hoped they weren't in pain.

After that I climbed in darkness with the lighted square of the laboratory getting smaller and smaller below me, like a night game beneath the Goodyear Blimp. That tower must have been some kind of whispering gallery because even at the top I continued to hear the creatures in the third cell.

But the top was far away from where I was at that moment. I climbed mechanically, without thinking about it. While my body did that I dumped out all the clues in my shoe box again, only this time they made a picture. It wasn't pretty, but it was just about complete.

Mr. Will had started bothering Whipper at about the same time as Max Toodemax sent his letter announcing that he was throwing everybody into the street. I forgave myself for not being tipped off by the timing; at that point I had no case, let alone suspicions. The credulity gas should have helped me along, but sometimes I can be kind of thick.

It wasn't until I had gone to see Mr. Knighten Daise about Mr. Will's high-toned list that the fog in my brain began to clear. Mr. Daise liked to hide in the bodies of animals because, he said, he had many enemies and this would throw them off. He might be right. I had dealt with him as a lobster and, most recently, as a camel. But that afternoon Mr. Daise had been in a reckless mood. He'd been human. And a very strange kind of human at that. He was no longer righteously indignant at Iron Will for somehow making every breeze whisper with a credulity gas breath; he even liked androids well enough to stop competing with them with his Surfing Samurai Robots.

Either somebody had gotten to Mr. Daise or

this wasn't him. Even then I was inclined to think it wasn't him. Irv Doewanit had told me that androids are grown from the cells of real people. Even in the shape of a camel Mr. Daise would still have human cells. The android grown from those cells would be human and look like the original article. Carla DeWilde or Whipper Will could have told me if my theory was right, but I didn't need them. I had a human at Mr. Daise's house drinking his hooch, and a camel in the lab beneath the Sign of the Times Sign Cemetery, a subsidiary of Will Industries. That told me all I wanted to know.

Seeing and talking to Max Toodemax at the neighborhood meeting, I began to understand what was going on. The hot air was wild and crazy that night, full of romance and credulity gas. Everybody felt it. Everybody would believe anything. Everybody but Mr. Toodemax. It helped that he had been wearing an outfit that covered his neck, but that was a clue I didn't really need.

Somebody was replacing important people with androids, growing them from sample cells. Eventually this person would have all his androids in position and he could run Los Angeles through them. He needed Whipper Will because this person didn't want his androids to go stale. The kidnapping of my friends had originally been in aid of forcing Whipper to work. The mastermind would also want to know why Zamp and the surfers weren't affected by the credulity gas. That would be important to him but not as important as making the replacements.

I had met three prominent men, all of whom wore suits every time I saw them, despite the event, despite the heat. Somewhere other than Los Angeles, that might not have meant anything, but here in laid-back Lala Land men didn't wear ties at any but the most formal occasions. Even so, by itself this business with the ties meant very little. But Iron Will had threatened his son and kidnapped his son's friends. Knighten Daise was human again and suddenly a great appreciator of androids. Max Toodemax wanted to make more money by putting up condos. Not like any of them. Not like them at all.

I looked at the way my picture fit together, enjoying it the way a tired housewife enjoys gazing at a drainer full of clean dishes. I enjoyed it now because I figured that later somebody might object to my enjoyment and object with force behind it. I put everything back into the shoe box and kept climbing.

I climbed for so long I thought maybe I'd missed the top. That was silly, of course, but I think a lot of silly things when I'm exhausted. I heard a noise and stopped. My limbs tingled and burned and felt no stronger than sausage links. My breath came quickly, taking in the smell of oil on the silver pillar and of the dry warm stones in the walls. The familiar insult of smog and the very faint sharpness of furniture wax prodded me.

The vague shuffling and hissing of Mr. Will's

failed experiments came up the chimney, but that wasn't what stopped me. The new noises came from above, the indistinct sound of polite conversation in words I could not make out.

It was one of the most difficult things I ever did, but I began to climb again. The conference room was closer than I'd thought, and I really did almost miss it because my eyes were closed. The ladder passed it, leaving me just enough room to get by. It must have been quite a squeeze for Danny. An authoritative male voice saying, "And so I said to the mayor . . ." stopped me. I opened my eyes.

I was on a level with the duct Danny Macabre had told me about. I hooked my arms around the ladder, leaned closer to the one slit that was a little wider than the others, and looked through.

The room was small for Will Industries, only big enough to hold a sock hop. Tasteful paintings of smoky shapes hung on the pigeon-gray walls. The table in the center of the room was a heavy glass slab shaped like the lid of a coffin. The wooden chairs had backs in the same shape. So did the thin blocks of paper at each place. The pencils were just pencils. The only other thing on the table was a model of a Melt-O-Mobile that was bigger than a bread box. Everybody looked good in the soft designer lighting.

Most of the men wore dark suits and shirts of varying shades of white—from hen's egg to oyster. Em Shannon was wearing what he always

wore for the papers, a pilly old tan sweater and
gray pants that made him look, from the waist
down, like an elephant. His dark hair was not
quite combed and his glasses were not quite on
straight. He probably had pens in a plastic
holder in his shirt pocket, but I couldn't see
them because of the sweater. The surfers would
have called him a full hank even if they'd known
he was worth eighty million bucks.

Three women were in the room. One of them
was Darken Stormy, looking like a disco god-
dess in a tight blue dress that sparkled when
she moved. The shoulders of the dress had come
off a Queen of Outer Space costume and the
front was cut in a deep V from here to a location just north of her navel. Most of the men
and at least one of the women had trouble not
staring. Her shoes matched her dress but the
buttons in her ears were flaming red, matching
her lips and the highlights in her hair. She gave
everybody her prizewinning smile as she offered drinks and round bits of food no larger
than quarters.

One of the other women was a blond bimbo
newscaster I'd seen on TV. She was dressed for
success in a dark suit and an incandescent
white blouse. When she glanced at Darken she
kind of sniffed, as if just being in the same room
offended her. The other woman was much older
and could have been a sister of the brunette
down in the cell. In her severely cut suit and
clunky brown shoes she looked like the princi-
pal at the school where the Little Rascals went.

She was too busy being one of the boys to worry about Darken's cleavage.

Everybody but Darken was on Mr. Will's exclusive list, and none of them had yet earned their checkmarks. Each of them would be useful in his or her own way as a puppet through which Los Angeles could be run.

Mr. Will was making the rounds, glad-handing people, buying them drinks, winking at Darken Stormy as if they shared some secret. Only it wasn't really Mr. Will. Mr. Will was on his way to room twenty-eight at the Shady Pines Motel. He had his tie off and anybody who wanted to could get a good look at his neck. Not like this Mr. Will here in the conference room, a Mr. Will wearing his tie knotted tight up under his chin to hide the blue plastic collar.

That was one of the things I didn't yet understand. If Mr. Will was behind all this, why had he replaced himself? If he wasn't, who was? And how had they gotten in so tight with Superhero Androids?

On the tick of ten-thirty the android Mr. Will marched to the head of the table and stood there with his fingertips on it. He called the meeting to order and everybody but Darken sat down. She hovered, filling glasses, taking away empty plates.

The android Mr. Will smiled. He did good work, but having recently seen the smile the real Mr. Will used, this one looked like a cartoon parody. He said, "Thank you all for coming. I think you will find that you have not wasted your time."

Polite interest from everyone but Em Shannon, who said, "I like a modest man." He got a dirty look from the bimbo newscaster and no applause. He frowned and sank into his seat like a clenching fist.

The android Mr. Will said, "As a matter of fact, Mr. Shannon, I *am* being modest. My offer will both astonish and excite you. You may turn me down, but if you do you will always wonder if you did the right thing." He waited for Em Shannon to make another clever comment. When he didn't the android Mr. Will went on. "Before I go any further, I must ask all of you, whatever your decisions, to swear never to reveal the subject of this meeting to anyone."

"Why?" a bald man asked. I think it was Anderson Charles, who owned a bank that owned half the city.

"Too many people would want what I am offering," the android Mr. Will said, "and I could not accommodate them. Besides, the government would probably want to regulate my activities, and that would be—" Mr. Will smiled with all the charm of a plaster flower, "—inconvenient. You will understand in a moment. Do you all agree?"

After a buildup like that, rocks would agree. Even Em Shannon nodded solemnly, as if being sworn in as an honorary deputy sheriff. I couldn't keep myself from nodding too.

Pleased at the impression he had made, the

android Mr. Will spoke further. "Superhero Androids has recently made a breakthrough. No longer will their androids go stale like so many loaves of bread. No longer will SA androids need to be periodically replaced. No longer will they be less than mortal." That smile again. "It is this breakthrough that allows me to offer you—" He paused like a magician enjoying the moment before he pulls the rabbit from the hat, "immortality." The android Mr. Will had everybody's attention. We had almost forgotten to breathe. I was leaving finger-shaped grooves in the ladder.

The android Mr. Will said, "I am not speaking metaphorically. For a fee that may seem exorbitant until you consider what you are getting, SA scientists will install your consciousness in the body of a vat-grown android, guaranteed to be immortal."

Darken was still smiling, a little smugly I thought. She had probably heard this spiel before. But the other faces had expressions mixed like vegetables in a bag of succotash. Mostly they looked dubious, as if they were not yet certain that someone in the room had not washed.

The old dame sat ramrod straight now, as if she'd been slapped and was trying not to give the slapper the satisfaction of seeing her react. The eyes of the bimbo newscaster opened wide enough to show red veins not normally seen on TV, then squinted as if studying out something in her head. Her hands shuffled phantom news copy. Em Shannon pretended to be bored, but when he reached for the glass of cola in front of him he almost missed it. He got his hands around it at last and threw the liquid back so fast he choked on it and began to cough. For a long time Em Shannon's coughing and Darken Stormy's motherly cooing were the only sounds in the room.

I don't know what expression was on my face, but the android Mr. Will had surprised me only a little. He had to offer something like that, of course. He couldn't expect people with good grips on their lives to let go just for his convenience. He would have to offer them something, and immortality was as good an exchange as any.

"No aging?" the bimbo newscaster said as if she were checking on the mileage of a used car.

"None," said the android Mr. Will.

The woman in the practical shoes stood up and gave the android Mr. Will a glare that should have set his hair on fire. Reining in her shaking voice, the woman said, "What you propose is at the very least immoral. It is probably unethical. It is certainly against the law."

"To live forever?" the android Mr. Will said, and laughed like an insurance agent.

"The old must give way to the young."

"Garbage. The weak must give way to the strong."

The others in the room watched the two go at it, surprisingly calm, trying to decide which side they were on. Em Shannon smiled in the way he must have when confronted with a new software problem.

The woman marched to the door. Only the android Mr. Will watched her. The others were busy with their own thoughts. Brows were wrinkled. Drinks were sipped. Pads were tapped with the tips of pencils. Before the woman could touch the doorknob, the android Mr. Will said, "Ms. Fergusson."

She stopped but she didn't turn around.

"I'd like to show you something."

She turned around and crossed her arms. Her eyebrows went up like the two halves of a drawbridge.

The android Mr. Will came around to the side of the table and reached between Mr. Charles and the blond newscaster to the model of the Melt-O-Mobile. His move was no more theatrical than the move a ditchdigger might make reaching for his shovel. It was economical and quick. It needed to get done and he didn't want anybody to question him about it.

The customers watched in fascination as the roof of the model began to fizz. Soon the unclean smell of credulity gas socked me, completely covering the smell of furniture polish and of everything else. I was not sick, but I was not happy either.

After a while the car was gone. Nobody but the android Mr. Will moved, and he only walked back to the head of the table. He looked around and nodded, enjoying the waxworks. Ms. Fergusson's eyebrows lowered.

The android Mr. Will said, "How do you feel, Ms. Fergusson?"

"I feel like a prisoner," she said angrily.

"I don't think so, Ms. Fergusson. You are delighted to be here. How do you feel now, Ms. Fergusson?"

"Delighted, I'm sure." Smiling, she made a lot of new wrinkles.

"All of you believe it would be a wonderful idea to have your minds installed into SA androids."

They all agreed with him. Everything he said was obvious. The sky was blue. Even Darken Stormy chimed in.

"You all feel in your bones that helping me run Los Angeles my way is the best way to spend the rest of your lives."

More nodding. More enthusiastic words of agreement.

The truth was, I had not been certain before that this Mr. Will was an android. Such things as evil twin brothers existed even when no one mentions them. But now I had evidence. Darken Stormy's neck was visible nearly to her belly button. No blue plastic collar. If any of the guests had been androids I don't think this Mr. Will would have bothered to invite them to his party. Yet credulity gas had been created. A Melt-O-Mobile couldn't create the gas alone, not even with smog present. Android cooties were necessary too. The cooties could have come from only one place. But why? How?

That wasn't nearly as important as what I was going to do next.

The android Mr. Will made up my mind for me. He said, "Darken, will you please take us down?"

"Of course, sir." She clicked to a wall on her spiky heels and pulled a painting away from it on hinges. Behind the painting were two buttons. She pushed the lower one. Suddenly the self-assured hum of heavy machinery kicked in. I didn't see any more in the room after that. I was too busy dropping down that ladder, trying not to be crushed to death.

26

The Dinosaur Waltz

As the room descended on the silver hydraulic pillar a giant gear wheel rolled down after me, its teeth fitting one by one into the spaces between the rungs of the ladder. It came just fast enough, maybe a little faster than that. I was in such a hurry I kept tangling myself in the rungs.

The floor was so far away it didn't seem to be getting any closer. I grabbed a rung with both hands and gripped the outside of the ladder's uprights with the insides of my feet. I slid, controlling my speed with my feet and my hands, more than once almost ripping my arms from their sockets. The big gear wheel stayed exactly three rungs above me all the way down. I dropped from four rungs up, hit the floor hard, and rolled out of the way. The floor of the conference room touched the floor of the laboratory with all the fuss of a pinfeather landing on a puddle. I backed around a bend in the wall and stood silently in a triangular shadow. It wasn't very dark, but if I kept still and nobody looked in my direction it might be enough.

The meeting room door opened, allowing a

cloud of credulity gas to escape. The crowd came out by ones and twos, with no more urgency than people leaving a movie theater. The android Mr. Will came last. He wasn't carrying a gun but his attitude said that he was a man in complete control.

I could have yelled then, told the guests what a terrible guy the android Mr. Will was, told them I was there for the rescue. But after I was done the android Mr. Will could tell them whatever *he* wanted, as he had back at the Convention Center. Then I could yell again. The crowd would believe one thing and then the other. The winner would be the man who lost his voice last. The solution wasn't elegant. Yelling would ultimately get me nowhere.

While I thought this Darken Stormy played nurse, helping the android Mr. Will take skin samples of each of them, put each sample into a round transparent dish, cover the dish, and put it into a refrigerator. The people joked a little, as people in line will. If I hadn't known they were under a sinister influence I would not have guessed.

"Come on, folks," the android Mr. Will said. "You'll like it in this nice cell."

They walked to the other side of the lab, where the android Mr. Will looked into the cells that had lately contained his other guests. With wide-open eyes and a half-open mouth he looked at what wasn't in them. Out loud he said, "Where are they?" His voice was a little strangled.

Darken stepped forward and helped him look. In the end cell one of the failures began to snort. A pig would have sounded more cultured.

The android Mr. Will glanced around quickly. His eyes swept over me but didn't stop. He hustled all his guests into one cell. Before he closed the door I stepped out of the shadow and said, "The jig is up. You'd better let them go." I had only the vaguest of plans and no gun, but I didn't think waiting longer would buy me anything. One of my hands was in a pocket. If I was lucky the android Mr. Will would make a wrong assumption about that.

Darken and the android Mr. Will jumped as if I'd stuck them with a pickle fork. The guests looked at me with surprise. The smell of credulity gas was thinning; perhaps it was thin enough that these people would believe the truth if they heard it. There was no way to know by just looking at them. I said, "I'm Zoot Marlowe. I'm here to help." Mr. Will swung the cell door shut and the loud clang made the lab vibrate like a bell.

Em Shannon and Ms. Fergusson and the others clumped up against the bars of the cell, all talking at once. The android Mr. Will told them to shut up and they did. "Let us out," Ms. Fergusson said.

The android Mr. Will didn't say anything, but eyed me as if wondering where to begin carving. I said, "She's right. You're in big trouble, but it could still go easier for you if you let them leave."

"Did you free the others?"

I shrugged and said, "I don't know why you just didn't kill them. You had samples. You could grow all the androids you wanted to."

The android Mr. Will went to stand behind a lab bench. He rested his fingertips on it the way he had on the glass table in the conference room. His hands looked like big pink spiders. Darken watched us while her lower lip twitched. She wanted to bite it again, but she had a lot of discipline. Nothing was more important than looking good.

The android Mr. Will actually smiled when he said, "You don't know much about androids, Mr. Marlowe. You can't grow an android from just one cell. You should be able to, but you can't. In order to grow replacement androids I needed more samples from the originals. Samples taken from androids don't work." The pink spiders did push-ups. "Of course, now that Whipper has fabricated an immortal android I don't need originals anymore."

Ms. Fergusson and the others looked horrified. Nobody had to tell them that if this guy didn't need them, they wouldn't be around long.

"Where are they?" the android Mr. Will said.

I said, "In a safe place," hoping I was right.

"No matter. I'll have to replace them again, but that's a minor annoyance. Unlike yourself." He strolled along the locked cells as he spoke. "You are not an annoyance at all." He glanced into the cell full of failed experiments, clucked like a chicken, and walked on.

Just killing time before it killed me, I said, "You don't seem like the kind of android Mr. Will would grow on purpose."

He was standing in front of the wall-mounted wooden box in which I had found the key to the cells. It fascinated him. He tore his eyes away and glanced at me, puzzled as if I had spoken to him in Gomkrix, the language we'd all spoken before English became so popular on T'toom. Then the smile broke out on his face like a rash. He said, "All this talk about androids has softened your brain, Marlowe. I am Iron Will, Whipper Will's father and the chief executive officer of Will Industries."

"Who was that guy in the cell? Your long-lost brother?"

It was his turn to shrug. He said, "Why not?" The idea appealed to him.

"Then you wouldn't mind removing your tie."

"What?"

"Look," I said. "I'll make this easy for you. When you pushed the button on that Melt-O-Mobile model you made credulity gas that you used to get those folks down here and into the cell. The Melt-O-Mobile can't make credulity gas by itself. It needs to fizz in the presence of smog and an android. Smog was in the conference room, probably piped in from outside. But Darken Stormy is obviously not an android. Your guests are not androids. *You* must be the android."

He nodded. We were two reasonable guys. He

said, "Let's say I am. Then what?" The smile was a little stiff now, but it remained attached.

"Actually, I was hoping you would tell me. I understand why you kept hostages. Until Whipper Will developed the immortal android you would need to keep them around for their cells. You'd need to grow new android accomplices every so often, not to mention growing your own occasional new body from the real Mr. Will's cells. What I don't understand is why Mr. Will grew you in the first place. He wouldn't need your help taking over Los Angeles."

The android Mr. Will laughed at that. It was a loud unpleasant sound, like a tin can going down a garbage disposal. It went on for a long time. We all stared at him: me, kind of whimsically; the gang behind bars, with barely suppressed horror; Darken, as if he'd used the wrong fork.

"You know, Marlowe, you're not very bright. I can only assume it was luck that led you here. Because you came without reinforcements, without weapons, armed only with a smart mouth and a matched set of wild theories."

"Not so wild," I said, knowing he was right about the rest of it. He spoke too casually now. Even if he really thought I was stupid I had figured out or guessed too much to be just left lying around. If he had been carrying a gun he'd have already used it. No gun, then. Nothing so clean and fast.

He unhooked the box from the wall and revealed a lever. Without saying another word or looking at me again, he pulled it.

A grating noise began and a section of the wall opened like a garage door. Even before the wall came all the way up I could smell the odor of the reptile house.

A creature came from behind the wall, so light on its feet that it nearly pranced. I had seen Disney's *Fantasia*, various versions of *The Lost World*, and a lot of other pictures that featured dinosaurs. The surfers liked monsters. This monster was small as such things went, barely larger than a horse. Its skin was a dull green with brighter highlights over the muscles. It walked on two legs and held before it hands that seemed ridiculously tiny and delicate. Its eyes had never heard of mercy, and its teeth were made for death. It was a vest-pocket tyrannosaurus rex and I was terrified.

The rex stopped next to the android Mr. Will, who reached up to slap one solid shoulder affectionately. A forked tongue lashed out from the mouth of death and went away. The android Mr. Will said, "This is a tyrannosaurus rex, the king of the dinosaurs." The android Mr. Will smiled. "We call him Elvis."

I was not moving. I was barely breathing. I may have blinked.

"After I take over Los Angeles, tyrannosaurs like Elvis will help me keep order. Dogs are boring. Tigers, even saber-toothed tigers, are not so impressive." Without raising his voice, the android Mr. Will said, "Kill, Elvis." The rex seemed to understand. Like a dancer, it stalked toward me.

I backed away, of course. I wanted to run, but I was certain that if I did the rex would be on me the way a cat is on a mouse and the show would be over but for the screaming. I slid back and back across the floor, the android Mr. Will following me and the rex like a referee—keeping close but not getting in the way. I don't know what Darken Stormy was doing.

I bumped against something hard. It was a lab bench. I backed around it till its width was between me and the rex. We watched each other across the table like a couple of billiard champions. Its fingers twitched and its tongue took another swipe at the air, then it came after me again.

I picked up a beaker and threw it at the rex. The beaker thumped off the rex's chest and crashed against the floor. The rex made a sound from before time and walked through the glass shards as if they were fallen leaves.

I could throw more glassware at it, but that would be harder on the glassware than it was on the rex. I wasn't worried about making it angry. It was angry already.

We circled another lab bench. The android Mr. Will called out, "Play him, Marlowe. He likes it." He laughed, sounding like something behind a padded door.

I passed the ladder and thought about squeezing around the big gear and up it. Not much room. Besides, going up when there was only one way down was too much like being trapped. Besides, while I was climbing the rex might decide to use my foot for a teething ring.

I feinted from side to side, which seemed to confuse the rex. It stopped, watching me, a little fascinated. Sure, I could keep it up for another few minutes before I got nauseous and tired. I could dance with the rex some more, backing into this and that, pitching bits of Mr. Will's expensive chemistry set. But the fact was there was no place to go. It was just a matter of endurance, and I knew too well who had more of that. I broke and ran.

Behind me the rex breathed and shuffled through broken glass. The sound was getting closer, but that was OK because I had a plan. I was not confident it would work, but it would keep me occupied while the rex got close enough to tear me into hamburger.

I backed into the side of the vat of android ur-glop. The wall was warm as blood and rose above my head the height of my body. The rex did not close in right away, but kind of circled around while it whipped its tongue at me and made occasional hissing sounds, as if it were inflated and air were escaping. It was enjoying itself. Nobody had given it a workout like this for a long time. Life was boring when all you did was live behind a wall and eat dino-chow.

With no more thought than a character in a play I slid sideways along the wall until I came to a ladder I knew had to be there. I turned around and began to climb with my head twisted so I could watch the rex approaching. I was halfway up before the rex reached the bottom of the ladder. It hung a single talon from a rung and narrowed its eyes to watch me. The rex was probably some kind of dinosaur genius because it figured out what to do. It climbed.

It rocked from side to side, having barely enough room between the ladder and the wall of the vat to get its toes over the rungs. It was ungainly, it was awkward, it was a joke, but it kept coming.

I reached the top of the ladder and walked out onto the catwalk that bridged the vat. It boomed like a drum head with every step I took. A thin silver cable threaded through uprights ran down each side, the only handrails. Below, android ur-glop bubbled and fell back onto itself. The stuff was an unhealthy white, the color of things that live under rocks, and had the pungent organic smell of food forgotten in the back of a refrigerator. The catwalk shook when the rex stepped onto it.

The android Mr. Will stood below looking up at us the way a kid looks at the star atop a Christmas tree. He said, "It's a natural-born killer, Marlowe. You can avoid it for a little while, but you can't escape."

I backed out to the middle of the catwalk with my hand on the thin silver cable. It was warm because of the muggy heat rising from the android ur-glop. The rex took small hops toward me, shaking the catwalk with each one. I watched the rex carefully and calculated exactly when it would have only one hop left before it leapt onto me and tore me apart like an old paper napkin. I watched. I'd never watched anything so hard in my life.

And then the rex made that last hop and then I reached out to it while it was still in the air and grabbed a small, ridiculously fragile wrist. At the same moment the android Mr. Will cried, "No!" and I swung the rex through the cable, snapping it. The rex howled in a prehistoric way, like a band saw cutting sheet tin. It hit the ur-glop hard, splashing some onto me. The rex thrashed around, melting as it did so, as it was reduced from a frightening monster to an unfinished soap sculpture to a suggestion of a lizard shape to nothing at all.

A long, narrow shape that could have been an arm or the remains of a tail beat against the surface one final time, flinging ur-glop over the side of the vat and onto the android Mr. Will. He screamed in a way that still gives me nightmares. One of the android failures joined in.

I ran to the end of the catwalk while ineffectually trying to clean myself with a handkerchief. Below, near the wall of the vat, the android Mr. Will was writhing under the vile android ur-glop like a creature being burned alive—arms waving high in the air, head thrown back, still screaming. He was melting. I never meant the android Mr. Will to be punished this way, but I couldn't stop it. I watched because I couldn't look away. He did not suffer long. In less than a minute all that was left of him was his clothes and a small white puddle of fizzing stuff that smelled like the stuff in the vat.

Darken Stormy came over and watched with me as the stuff stopped fizzing. Without looking at her I said, "That's the end of that, I guess."

"The end," she said.

The way she said it made me look at her. When I did I suddenly felt very tired. A pistol was in her hand and it was pointing at me. There was only one thing for me to do. It was corny, a cliché, but necessary. I put up my hands.

27

Fully Equipped

Her hand shook, but not enough. She wasn't nervous but angry. She said, "You've ruined everything."

"I thought I was making it all better."

"One quip too many," she said. And then again, more softly. The pistol steadied.

I don't like to upset people who have my life in their hands, so I said politely, "How have I ruined everything?"

Her face pinched together, getting as ugly as it could ever be. She looked like a little girl who had been too long at the fair and still was angry about going home. The hand holding the pistol didn't seem to be part of her; it was a statue's hand, hard, motionless, watching me with the pistol's single eye. I took a step back, hoping the motion looked natural, just something somebody would do while standing around talking. The pistol didn't move but it didn't go off either.

"He promised me immortality. Eternal life. Eternal beauty."

"Who did?"

"Mr. Will, of course."

I took another step back. She followed, but it was just a natural social move. She didn't think anything of it. I backed up more whenever I thought I could get away with it.

"Which Mr. Will?"

"What do you mean? Oh. The android. He promised to make me immortal and we would run Los Angeles together through the other androids, and now you've ruined everything. I'll never get my android body."

"And Los Angeles will have to take care of itself. I'm sorry," I said, trying hard to sound as if I meant it. "But maybe it's all for the best. I wouldn't want to spend the rest of eternity in a body made of glop."

"Easier than being a vampire." She went ahead and bit her lip. She had been right to fight it. Lipstick got onto her teeth and smudged her skin. The red looked just as sloppy and unsanitary as it would look on anybody else. "And the real Mr. Will will probably fire me."

"Well," I said, "you probably won't have much time to work for him anyway. The police will probably insist on monopolizing you."

"The police? Why?" The pistol rose and fell like a dinghy on a lake. I stepped back. We were halfway across the floor now and she didn't seem to have noticed. I was the center of Darken Stormy's attention.

"Short memory, Darken. Irv Doewanit is dead, remember?"

"I'm sorry about your friend, Mr. Marlowe, but I didn't kill him."

"Danny Macabre isn't so sure. He guided me down here in exchange for my not telling the police about your connection to the 'Surf City' music box."

She bit her lip again, but her gun hand was as steady as ever. She might have been modeling guns. "Poor Danny," she said, caressing his memory with the words. Then she was back with me. She said, "How did you find him?"

"I'm a detecting professional."

That made her smile. It was a nice smile even with lipstick all over it. She said, "I didn't kill him, Mr. Marlowe, or even order it done. I suppose it was silly of me, but I wanted that music box. Mr. Will the android said he'd help me get it. He sent an android to Whipper's house and found your friend there. Your friend made a mistake and got in the android's way. The android was a bodyguard model and not bred for subtlety. There was a struggle. Your friend was just something between the android and its assignment. Killing him was an accident. That's all."

"You could be sorry."

"We both have a lot to be sorry about."

By this time I was leaning against the jamb of the conference room door. Gas from the evaporated Melt-O-Mobile hung in the smoggy air like bad feelings and mixed with the cooties from the android ur-glop that had splashed on me. The vague smell of credulity gas got stronger.

I backed into the room and sat in one of the chairs that had a back like the lid of a coffin. Darken stood over me with her pistol. From that distance a blind man could not have missed.

Darken said, "Good-bye, Mr. Marlowe." She made a stable stance by spreading her legs tight against her dress, and held her pistol in both hands. She aimed it at me.

I said, "I'm your friend, Darken. You don't want to shoot me."

Doubt crossed her eyes like a shadow over water, but she lowered the gun and gave me her big smile. "Mr. Marlowe," she said as if she were making a big profit by selling me back my own teeth.

"Come on, Darken," I said. "Let's get out of this smell."

"Right."

She let me take the gun away from her and we strolled across the lab to the cell where the A party was stashed. I moved her along pretty fast, not knowing when the credulity gas would wear off.

"Get us out of here," Anderson Charles said, a nasty whine in his voice.

I found the big key in the wooden box the android Mr. Will had taken off the wall and came back with it. I opened the cell and the guests streamed out. I guided Darken Stormy into the cell and locked the door. Not worried, just curious, she said, "What am I doing in here?"

"You'll be happy," I said.

She nodded, looking around as if appreciating the sultan's palace.

I went to where the movers and shakers had clotted in the walkway between two lab benches. They all tried to shake my hands at once. When I ran out of hands the rest patted me on the back. I would have let them continue but I still had questions. The answers were not down here. Besides, the place made me nervous. Too much death was down here. Too many mistakes had been made and not paid for.

As I herded my crowd toward the curtain with the horse on it Darken called after us, "Marlowe, you bastard."

We stopped and looked back at Darken. She was gripping the bars. Her head could not quite fit between them. "Let me out."

"You're happy," I told her.

"Like hell I am."

"Somebody will be back for you soon."

She was a nice woman who was too pretty for her own good—pretty enough that she thought beauty was all she had going for her. So she'd conspired with somebody who'd promised her that she would never lose it. She didn't mind that she had helped kidnap people and get people murdered. It didn't matter that the intention of her employer was to take over a city and use dinosaurs to keep people in line. Nothing mattered but her beauty. I felt a little sorry for her but not much. Everybody has problems, and being a dish did not seem as bad as some others I'd heard about.

She was still shouting my name as I ducked behind the thick curtain with the horned horse on it.

Once my crowd entered the long stone tunnel they began to complain. They wanted to go back the way they had come—through the civilized front door where VIPs enter. But the android Mr. Will had stationed guards up there. People had to sign in and out. It was all very clean and official. I thought Danny Macabre's back door would be easier to deal with despite the dirt and the darkness and the strange noises, and I told them so. Only partly convinced, they moved on but they continued to grumble.

On our way through the locker room we met a very thin old man with wisps of cotton on his head that may have been hair. He had a towel in one hand and a bottle of shampoo in the other. In-between he was naked. When he saw us his eyebrows went up and he gasped and ran away, his towel covering his ass. The newscaster bimbo made a cynical smile. I told Ms. Fergusson she could open her eyes.

When I stepped into the corridor behind the wall mirror, it was darker than I remembered it. We had no flashlight—the android Mr. Will had been right about my not being prepared—but after the lights behind my eyes stopped popping I could see a surprising amount of light that filtered in from the top and sides, giving the place the grainy look of an old movie.

After that it was easy. Just a quick walk along

the Civil Defense tunnel and up through the trapdoor under the BONANZA FEED AND GRAIN sign. I was hoping to sneak across the street without talking to Danny Macabre, but he was leaning against the outside of his tiny shack of an office waiting for us.

My people were looking around at the signs, surprised at where we had come up, when Danny approached, smiling. While his eyes searched the crowd his smile collapsed like an ice-cream cone under a fat man and he said, "Where is she?"

"Down there," I said. I was weary, even more weary than I had been when Darken Stormy had pulled a gun on me. A lot had happened since then.

"Why? Is she OK?"

"She's fine. With her looks, even after she's arrested she'll probably be fine. Besides, *she* didn't kill anybody."

He looked in the direction of the trapdoor and I said, "Don't even think about helping her escape. Right now she has a chance. If she runs away her chance will make a caraway seed look like a watermelon."

Danny thought about that, then grumbled, "Damned music box," as if he were alone.

I agreed with him, walked past the two limousines and out the gate. My crowd followed me. While we waited for the traffic to clear I looked back and saw Danny standing in the same place, moving his head as if trying to locate the source of a strange noise.

* * *

Room twenty-eight of the Shady Pines Motel looked like backstage at the circus. People were sprawled across the two king-sized beds; others sat on the floor. Flopsie and Mopsie sat on the sink counter. Hanger had found a candy bar somewhere and was trying to feed it to Mr. Daise. He kept telling her to stop but she wouldn't. Nobody but Hanger and Mr. Daise were talking. Everybody in the room had the empty eyes of people waiting for a bus. Bill was in a corner as still as he'd be if I'd turned him off. I wondered if the woman at the desk had seen these people come in. I wondered if she cared.

When I came in with more people Hanger stopped what she was doing. Zamp stood up. Everybody looked at us. Then the dam broke and the reunion began. All these exclusive people knew each other. Maybe they wouldn't see each other for months or years at a time. Maybe they didn't even like each other much. But they'd all come through the fire together and that did things to people. They greeted each other like family.

The surfers gathered around me, and Bill brought me the room key and said, "Some party, huh, Boss?"

I agreed that it was, told the surfers how bitchen it was to see them again. Zamp and I briefly touched noses.

"You OK?" Zamp said.

"I'm tired."

"Let's go home."

I didn't ask him whether he meant Malibu or T'toom. At the moment it didn't matter as long as nobody pulled a gun or a dinosaur on me. I said, "I have something to do first."

I stepped across the minefield of people to where Mr. Will was sitting on a bed next to Bingo. Bingo hugged me and sat back down. She patted Mr. Will's hand. He'd lost his tie, and his shirt was spotted with dirt. Mr. Will saw me coming and came to meet me. We shook hands and he said, "I don't know how you found us, sir, but I am delighted." He winked. "We could use a man like you in plant security."

"Not just now, Mr. Will. But you can answer a question for me." Conversations exploded around us like fireworks. Bingo watched us, hungry to hear what we had to say. Nobody else was any more interested than the table lamps.

"Anything." He looked as if he meant it.

I said, "Where did that android come from?"

Mr. Will turned a nice rosy pink. He glanced at Bingo but wouldn't look either of us in the eye.

I said, "You must have had something in mind besides he should take over your life."

Words rushed out of him. He said, "I wanted to be immortal."

I nodded. I could almost finish his story now, but I wanted to hear it from him.

When I didn't say anything he went on. "I grew an android of myself, hoping that I could put my consciousness into it."

"Androids don't last long enough to be immortal."

"I thought maybe my son Whipper would help with that. If Bingo is hugging you, you probably know Whipper?"

"We've met. Go on."

"As you've probably guessed, something went wrong. The android took over, just like an evil twin in a pulp magazine." He shook his head and laughed a little at his own foolishness. "I had a lot of time to think in that cell. I'm going out of the android business. I don't want what happened to me to happen again." He pointed at Mr. Daise, now chewing on something with an energetic sideways motion. Hanger stood nearby smiling, so it was probably the candy bar. Mr. Will said, "Mr. Daise and I have been talking. He's invited me to be on the board of directors of Surfing Samurai Robots."

I thought about two egos that size in one room and the fights they would have when the glow of their rescue wore off. I said, "That's fine. What about those things in that third cell?"

Mr. Will shook his head. "They'll decompose soon. I'll see that they're taken care of till that happens."

The party continued around us.

Bingo said, "Darken Stormy is not really a bad person, you know."

"No," I said. "She just made some bad friends." She also wouldn't be young forever. We both looked at Mr. Will.

He shrugged and said, "I guess that if she needs a lawyer, she'll have the best."

Bingo kissed him on the cheek. I couldn't beat that with anything, so I didn't try. Instead I said, "What about the credulity gas?"

Mr. Will shook his head. "Another bad by-product of the android business. Another reason to stop. Credulity gas was created by accident. I was going to find out what was going on and stop it, but my android threw me into the sneezer before I had a chance."

"You and Mr. Daise'll do fine," I said.

It was a little intimate, but there was enough room in the two limousines for all the exclusive people. Mr. Will drove one and the newscaster bimbo drove the other. Mr. Daise, in camel mode, loped alongside. I don't know where they went but it was far away from the Sign of the Times Sign Cemetery.

I took Zamp and Bill and the surfers home. It was another hot day, and the freeways were full of cars containing people who had called in sick so they could go to the beach. The drive west was long and sweaty, and though the car was very crowded nobody complained. Bingo said that after all that time in a dungeon the outside world was overwhelming and seemed a little fake. Just watching it took all your energy and concentration.

After a while the traffic got heavier and the air got cooler. I had plenty of time to think but I didn't do it. I had only one question left, and as far as I could tell, there was no way to figure out an answer. Only Whipper could fix me up. Either he would or he wouldn't.

When we arrived in Malibu he met us at the door. His father had found out he was working at Willville and had sent him home, more or less permanently. Not everything was straight between them, but they both wanted to talk.

The surfers sat around the living room getting used to being home. I went to the hall closet, took a breath, and opened the door.

"Clothes, Boss," Bill said.

"Yeah." On the floor was a pile of stuff that looked like erasure rubbings—all that was left of the android Zamp.

I found Whipper in the kitchen with Bingo and the real Zamp. Bill hopped onto the counter and swung his legs. As I sat down I heard a Gino and Darlene movie begin on the TV. Everybody has a different idea of comfort.

We sat nodding at each other. Bingo put out four brewskies and for a while they took our entire attention. The cold flow cut through tension and fear. No. The brewski was cold and it tasted good, but it would take more than a little alcohol to loosen the kinks in my back.

Whipper said, "You pulled it out again, Zoot. You gnarly dude."

"Gnarly, cool, and bitchen. But I still need a question answered."

"Ask away, Holmes."

"Did anybody ever find out why you and the

other surfers weren't affected by the credulity gas?"

Whipper took a big swallow of his brewski. He went on so long I almost took the can away from him. But at last he lowered it and said, "I found out. It's the yoyogurt."

Bingo and Zamp and I looked at him with surprise. Then we laughed. I could have figured it out after all. The fact that the surfers ate yoyogurt was probably the only thing about them that was different from everybody else in this case.

Whipper said, "What about you, Zoot?"

"What about me?"

"You know all about me now. What about you?"

"Let's just say that if you thought Bay City is a lot farther away than Santa Monica, you wouldn't be wrong."

"You got that right," Bingo said.

We sipped some more till Whipper said, "What happened at the neighborhood meeting?"

I was about to answer when Bingo said, "It doesn't matter."

When we'd all put down our cans and were looking at her, she said, "I had a long talk with Max Toodemax in the motel room."

"Motel room?" Whipper said, very curious.

Zamp told him it was a long story.

While Bingo told the long story to Whipper I walked outside with Bill and Zamp. The Sun hung about halfway up the sky, shining onto the crowded beach. Wind blew a smell of the sea at us, without a hint of credulity gas. Products would have to rise or fall on their advertising or, in a pinch, on their merit.

Zamp said, "What now?"

"Now," I said as I sat on the brick wall that divided Whipper's private deck from the public walkway, "I want to see Bill's brochure."

"Sure, Boss," Bill said. He opened a door in his side and handed me a folded piece of slick paper. "I'm fully equipped."

"I'll bet you are."

I unfolded the garish sheet. Zamp and I leaned together over it while Bill watched us with something in his eyes that I can describe only as pride.